I0657342

Thomas Wilson Reid

Gabrielle Stuart

Vol. 1

Thomas Wilson Reid

Gabrielle Stuart
Vol. 1

ISBN/EAN: 9783337347307

Printed in Europe, USA, Canada, Australia, Japan

Cover: Foto ©Andreas Hilbeck / pixelio.de

More available books at **www.hansebooks.com**

GABRIELLE STUART;

OR,

THE FLOWER OF GREENAN.

A Scottish Romance.

By THOMAS WILSON REID,

COMPILER OF THE "NEWSPAPER READER," AUTHOR OF "A STRUGGLE
FOR LIFE," ETC., ETC.

IN TWO VOLS.—VOL. I.

EDINBURGH:

THOS. GRAY & CO., 13 GEORGE STREET.

AYR: A. FERGUSSON, 18 HIGH STREET.

1882.

All Rights Reserved.

EDINBURGH :
PRINTED BY THOS. GRAY AND CO.

PREFACE.

IN venturing to offer the present two volumes to the public—which I trust will be a not too critical one—I have to apologise for not a few breaches of historical accuracy. I have taken the liberty of "shifting" a number of my scenes. But there is nothing I have written, even when it may seem to be purely fictitious, that is not founded on actual fact, or on the fact that general credence has long been, and even still is, given to the occurrences detailed.

The romance—if romance it can be properly called—is an endeavour to describe the state of matters, domestic and social, that existed in Scotland during a portion of the sixteenth century. More especially, however, is it an attempt to depict life and manners as they were in the West of Scotland at that period. Being a native of the town of Ayr, I have laid the main portion of my scenes in, and taken the great proportion of my characters from, that now famous town and its immediate locality.

For the many promises of support that I have received in the matter of subscription to the romance I am heartily grateful. Not a few leading Scottish families, especially in the western counties, have subscribed to the work; whilst in the English metropolis a Committee of London Scotsmen has been formed for the purpose of bringing "Gabrielle Stuart" under the notice of our countrymen there.

T. W. R.

London, *October* 1882.

TO

HARRY FINDLATER BUSSEY,

AND HIS BROTHER

BERNARD,

FOR KIND AND MATERIAL ASSISTANCE IN CARRYING OUT
SOME OF ITS DETAILS,

THIS WORK IS RESPECTFULLY DEDICATED

BY

The Author.

GABRIELLE STUART;

OR,

THE FLOWER OF GREENAN.

———◆———

CHAPTER I.

THE STORM—THE RESCUE.

" Mirk and rainy is the nicht ;
    No' a starn in a' the carie ;
Lightnings gleam athwart the lift,
    And winds drive wi' winter's fury."

Tannahill.

" IT is an awful night," was the involuntary
exclamation of William Park, a pilot
of the Port of Ayr, one dark November night
in the year 16—, when a dreadful storm had
lashed the Firth of Clyde into a terrible fury.
It was indeed an awful night. The relent-
less sea dashed itself madly on the trembling
shore. The wind roared, thunder rolled, and
rain fell in torrents.

Now and again a vivid flash of lightning would clearly disclose the far-distant hills of Arran, the frowning Ailsa Craig, and the still nearer Lady Isle, where, notwithstanding the fierce war of the elements, high revelry was being held in the once famous and well-frequented Castle on the little island.

It was the twenty-first anniversary of the birth of the brave but unfortunately dissipated Lord Kennedy of Greenan, and a large party of guests, under the charge of Park, the pilot, had been landed that afternoon on " the Leddy," as the romantic island was then and is now familiarly called.

Lady Isle is an insignificant little island lying in the fairway of the Firth of Clyde, about seven miles from Ayr. It is now divested of all buildings save a tall tower, which acts as a beacon for mariners navigating their ships between Glasgow and the Atlantic.

Park's trim schooner was gallantly riding out the fierce gale on the lee side of the island, which in these days was the scene of many a festive gathering. But there was no bodily or mental rest for the watchful pilot. He felt a presentiment of coming evil. In his case, as Schiller has well said, the throb of the heart was the voice of fate. As he nervously paced the deck of his stout little vessel he peered anxiously into the black gloom on every side.

Ever and anon Park thought he heard cries of distress, but he could discover nothing on the seething waters. At last a brilliant flash of lightning showed him that a pretty large but entirely dismasted ship was being driven headlong on the almost barren and always dimly-lighted island. Nearer and nearer came the doomed vessel. Then was heard one fearful crash, a loud and heartrending shriek,

> " The bubbling cry ;
> Of some strong swimmer in his agony; "

but nought was heard again save the howl of the tempest and the sound of the foaming sea dashing furiously against the rocky beach.

It was indeed a dreadful night, a night

which brought fear even into the brave heart of an experienced seaman like Pilot Park.

"Watch, ahoy!" suddenly shouted the pilot. "Bear a hand here with a boathook : something bearing down on us from the windward."

Quickly the watch is at hand, and a dripping bundle, tied to an oar, is at once snatched from the top of a mountainous wave.

What can the bundle be ? A shrill sound soon settles the question. It is the cry of an infant. Park, the pilot, had rescued from the angry sea a pretty girl not much more than six months old. Hastily he took the child to his cabin, and divested it of the wet clothing that clung to its body. Through its tears the infant smiled on the bluff sailor, and his heart became filled with compassion for the unfortunate being. But what is he to do with the frail creature ? He has no means of keeping it alive.

"Better," thought Pilot Park, "that the

child had perished among the waves of the sea than that it should be starved to death on board my schooner."

And then he discovered a little document pinned to the child's dress. But it was in a language the sensible but illiterate pilot did not understand. "*En Dieu est ma fiance.*— Marie." That was all. The poor mother, before launching her beauteous babe on the foaming billows, had only time to say that she put her trust in the Almighty.

By some means or other, as the pilot naturally concluded, the child should be taken ashore. It must speedily have female attention if its life was to be saved. So the sturdy seaman at once determined to take the infant to the island, and get it cared for. With some difficulty a boat was launched, and in a brief space—the child having been roughly rolled in a blanket—the pilot jumped on shore, carrying his precious burden in his brawny arms.

As rapidly as the storm would permit him, Park proceeded to the Castle on the middle of the island. Without experiencing any difficulty he walked through the great hall and direct to the ball-room, from which were plainly heard the merry sounds of music. Going at once to the handsome and youthful Lord Kennedy, the pilot pointed to the infant, while he handed his Lordship the document that had been attached to its clothes.

Slowly his Lordship read, "*En Dieu est ma fiance,*" but when he came to the name "Marie" he suddenly fell on the floor as if he had been struck stone dead.

All at once the dancing ceased, and a scene of the wildest confusion followed. From mouth to mouth the question went, "What means this?" but no one present was able to answer.

"When and where got you the child, Captain?" was the question repeatedly put to Park; but Park, at once suspecting that there might be something underlying all the confusion, answered not. "I'm too old an Ayr bird," said he internally, "to be caught by curious chaff; so I'll just spread my wings and fly back to my schooner." Which he accordingly did.

Fortunately, there was medical assistance at hand, and Lord Kennedy was lifted up and carried to his private chamber. The paper, on which was written the French sentence, was carefully appropriated by Jules, his lordship's French valet, while the infant foundling was affectionately tended by one of the domestics, a matron who herself had brought up a large family of children.

Naturally enough, as already stated, the revelry at once ceased throughout the Castle. For a considerable time there was nought but speculation concerning the strange and untoward circumstance that had so suddenly brought the coming-of-age festivities to a sad and untimely close; but it was not very long before the members of the brilliant company dispersed to the various apartments provided for their sleeping accommodation.

In the morning it was officially announced that Lord Kennedy was in a state of fever, and that his case was critical in the extreme.

His Lordship had been delirious during the early hours of the morning, and although not a few of those forming the previous night's company offered their cordial assistance in the alarming extremity, their attentions were respectfully declined, his Lordship's valet having sent a notice to the effect that he and the medical attendant would alone see to the welfare of Lord Kennedy.

It had been previously arranged that the guests should remain on the island for several days, but in the unfortunate circumstances, and the storm of the preceding night having materially abated, the majority of the company were rowed in small boats to the schooner which had* previously conveyed them to the Lady Isle, and in a brief space of time Pilot Park was steering his steady craft with its disappointed passengers towards the ancient and important port of Ayr.

Meanwhile we shall, for a moment, cut the thread of our intended tale, for the purpose of briefly describing the then town of Ayr, long ago famous in commercial history, and in modern days made still more famous as being the birthplace of the immortal Burns —a poet whose fame has extended to all parts of the known world, and whose centenary was more universally celebrated than that of any other known author. In India, China, and Japan; in the burning wilds of Africa, and throughout America; in our Australian Colonies, and in every country in Europe, the 25th of January 1859 was devoted, in whole or in part, to the celebration of the centenary of Robert Burns. Why this celebration was so wide-spread has been matter of considerable comment and of no little dispute. Yet the fact stands boldly out that no such universal honour was ever accorded to the memory of either poet or prose writer.

CHAPTER II.

" AULD AYR."

" Low, in a sandy valley spread,
　An ancient burgh reared her head;
　Still, as in Scottish story read,
　　She boasts a race
　To every nobler virtue bred,
　　And polish'd grace."

AT the period of which our tale is intended
to treat, the town of Ayr was not, in
any sense, like the Ayr of the present day.
Indeed, it was as unlike it as can possibly
be imagined. The houses were mainly small
thatched residences, the general buying and
selling trade of the town being carried on in
the open streets — if, indeed, narrow and
crooked alleys may be designated open
streets.

It is true, the " Auld Brig " was in existence, and had been so for perhaps thirty or
forty years; but, as far as we know, there is

no accurate record of the exact period when the once strong and now ancient structure was built. Its endurance was wonderfully well and strangely-prophetically illustrated by Burns, considerably more than a century later, when he made the Auld Brig say to the New—

"And though wi' crazy eild I'm sair forfairn,
I'll be a brig when ye're a shapeless cairn!"

But common folks, to save the toll which was then, and naturally enough, levied, preferred to cross the river by means of "the ford." And a dangerous ford it was. When the river was in "spate," as it not unfrequently was, especially in winter, lives were often lost in attempts to pass among the rapidly-rushing waters.

Ayr had long been a centre for the many military operations of the period. During the Scottish wars of independence the town eternally bristled with troops. The inhabitants being thus of a warlike character, the agriculture of the district was very backward indeed, and continued so for about a century and a-half after the period to which our tale relates. Thus the old rhyme was doubtless engendered—

" Kyle for a man,
   Carrick for a coo,
   Cunningham for butter and cheese,
   Galloway for woo'."

As early as the end of the twelfth or the beginning of the thirteenth century, Ayr was made a royal burgh by William the Lion. Kyle—that is, the district lying between the River Doon and the River Irvine, and, of course, embracing the town of Ayr itself— was the scene of the first grand exploits of the great Sir William Wallace, of whom there are not a few records in the town and its neighbourhood.

At the time of which we write, the Wallace Tower—then commonly known as the " Auld Tower "—was private property, belonging to the Cathcarts, a famous fighting family of the town. But it had not the slightest resemblance to the Wallace Tower of the present day, which is little more than fifty years old. Originally, the structure was a huge square two-storey building, its walls being of immense thickness and strength.

The little harbour of Ayr was, at that time, of considerable importance. Glasgow had not then risen to anything like its present great commercial eminence, and Greenock was comparatively unknown; the consequence was that French wines and other foreign imports were, as a rule, brought to the Port of Ayr, and thence forwarded by high road to all parts of Scotland.

Then there was the Castle of Ayr and the Fort or Citadel—Cromwell's Fort, as it was long called—and its neighbouring building, the Church of St John the Divine, a religious edifice that has long since disappeared. Moreover, on the north side of the river there arose the famous Newton Castle, which stood in close proximity to the Auld Brig, and was then the principal residence of the Craigie family, also a family of fighting fame. Besides the castles that have been named as existing in the old and new towns, there was, at the

time, some two or three miles along the
south shore, the strongly-fortified and well-ap-
pointed Castle of Greenan, one of the strong-
holds of the famous Kyle Kennedys—now a
little-frequented ruin, familiarly known in
the district as " Greenan Castle."

These particulars as to some of the ancient
and almost obsolete buildings of Auld Ayr
are given as being necessary to the carrying
out of part of the details of the present
story.   Return we now to some of the
characters already so briefly and imperfectly
introduced.

  . . . . .

Lord Kennedy had returned to the ances-
tral residence of Greenan.   His youth and
strong constitution had tided him over the
more dangerous part of a shock that would
have ended the days of many a weaker man ;
but he was still in a condition that required
all the care and skill of an eminent physician.
And Ayr could then boast, as often since it
has been able to do, of possessing the best
medical men out of Edinburgh and Glasgow

—men who then successfully combined bar-
bering with blood-letting.

In a room furnished with all the luxuries
of which the time could boast—and they
were not few—Lord Kennedy lay extended
on a couch. He looked pale and ill. Touching a gong that hung by the side of his couch,
he gave the signal for the appearance of
Jules, the French valet already mentioned.

"Has Park, the pilot, not yet arrived?"
peevishly demanded the sick man, as he
languidly turned himself round.

Receiving a reply in the negative, he
authoritatively said, "Let a messenger be
at once despatched for him."

After the lapse of little more than an
hour, Park was obsequiously announced by
Jules.

"Let him enter," said his Lordship, "and
see thou, varlet, that we are not in any
way disturbed."

Straw hat in hand, the blunt sailor entered,
and made his rough obeisance to Lord
Kennedy, who silently indicated that Park

was to take a seat near the foot of the couch.

"Where found'st thou the child on the night of the festivities at Lady Isle?" asked Lord Kennedy sternly.

"Tied to an oar, it was passing by my schooner, and so near that I was enabled to snatch it from the heaving waves."

"I have been told," resumed his Lordship, "that thou saw a shipwreck on the island on that same dreadful night."

"I did, my Lord, and I have since learned that she was a French barque, laden with wine for the port of Ayr."

"Did not all on board perish?" And the nobleman gazed fixedly at the pilot.

"I fancy they did; yet methinks that in the early morning I descried a strange-looking ship's boat being driven up the Firth, but she soon disappeared from my gaze."

"Well, Park, thou did'st act bravely and humanely in saving the child's life. But what say the good folks of the town regarding the circumstances of that night?"

Park hesitated to reply. He knew from experience the hasty temper and violent character of his employer.

"Speak out, man; be not afraid. I care not what they say."

"Emissaries, my Lord, from the Craufurds have been making inquiries at my house and elsewhere as to the nature of the document that was attached to the child's dress."

"Well, anything more?" almost eagerly demanded Lord Kennedy.

"They say that the writing on the paper having been in French, and your Lordship's sudden illness after reading it, must have something to do, not only with the child, but with your hasty return from Paris twelve months ago."

"Illogical louts! What care I for their scandalous tongues? But listen, Park. Keep thine own counsel. Thou knowest I can punish as well as reward."

Park knew this full well, for Lord Kennedy was as liberal as he was vindictive.

A pause then took place in the conversation.

Suddenly his Lordship said, "I have a commission for thee, Park. Thy schooner must be ready before dark to-night. The child must be taken to Glasgow, where I have arranged that it shall be cared for by a female friend of my man-servant, Jules. Thou must sail to-night after taking the child with its present nurse and Jules on board. Woman and child are now at Marling's Home Farm. And see," added his Lordship, significantly, as he handed Park a well-filled purse of gold pieces, "that thou rememberest what I told thee. Keep thine own counsel, and all will be well with thee in the future."

"Your Lordship's orders will be carried out to the letter," said Park, as he rose to depart on his secret mission.

"Stay," said Lord Kennedy, with affected carelessness. "How do the scandal-mongers know that the silly document was written in French? It is not a language with which many in the town or county are intimate."

"They have been told that the writing

was in a foreign language, and they now know that the wrecked vessel was a French wine ship."

"That is sufficient, Park. See thou Jules before thou goest from the Castle, and arrange the hour of embarkation with him."

Park again bowed obeisance, thanked his noble employer and retired.

Shortly afterwards Jules, his Lordship's wily confidant, was hastily summoned to his master's presence.

"See that the woman and child are, with sufficient secrecy, conveyed to the port of Ayr. Follow the track of the Roman Road, by the river; and mind that thou pratest not with any one on the way. Leave thy silly French and stupidly-talkative politeness aside for once, or it may be worse for thee."

"*Certainement, milord,*" answered the wily Frenchman, as he bowed gracefully.

"A truce, I say, with thy language and thy posturing. When thou reachest Glasgow thou alone must take the infant to thy friend's dwelling. Say it is thine own child, and that thou wilt call occasionally and see to its welfare."

With all a Frenchman's so-called instinctive politeness—although he had just been cautioned against it—Jules again bowed gracefully and withdrew.

.   .   .   .   .

That night saw Park's schooner scudding merrily up the Firth; the next day saw her at the now famous Tail o' the Bank ; while late on the night following the child of the waters was deposited, in parcel fashion, with a poverty-stricken woman in old Glasgow.

CHAPTER III.

THE STROLLING MINSTREL.

"No earthly clinging, no lingering gaze,
  No strife at her parting, no sore amaze;
  But sweetly, gently, she passed away
  From the world's dim twilight to endless day."

Anon.

SIX years and upwards had elapsed since
the night of the festivities on the Lady
Isle.   Lord Kennedy had been more than six
years married to the gentle Lady Edith,
daughter of the fierce Earl of Hamilton.
The marriage had been a hurried one, and
one of policy.   No children had blessed the
union, and the marriage was popularly considered to be an unhappy one.

Lord Kennedy's father had been slain in a
feud with the Craufurds, and he himself was
frequently absent from Greenan for months at
a time, taking part in the state and local
quarrels and battles that were so dreadfully

common at that unsettled period; while Lady Kennedy pined away at home, her time being principally spent in acts of religious devotion and deeds of charity.

Since the night of the coming-of-age festivities on Lady Isle, it had been long observed that Lord Kennedy was much changed. His once open and smiling, although somewhat debauched, countenance now showed a settled and bitter melancholy, and he looked ten years older than he really was.

One cool summer evening a group of idlers were collected at the Malt Cross of Ayr. The Cross then stood near the bottom of the Sandgate; and it is to be regretted that when it was removed in 1785 it was not re-erected on some eligible site, for the Malt Cross was really a fine specimen of ancient architecture.

The members of the somewhat motley crowd—half soldier, half civilian—collected in the neighbourhood of the Malt Cross were alternately criticising and admiring the performances of a meanly-clad woman who, with

a strong foreign accent, was singing a somewhat plaintive song, and accompanying herself on the lute. Poor woman! she had the
hectic flush of ill-health on her otherwise pale
and evidently once beautiful face.

After receiving from some of the crowd a
few of the huge and not very plentiful coppers
of the period, the musician accosted a young
and somewhat rough farmer-looking fellow,
with a great sword slung over his shoulders
(for in those troublous times all men, gentle
and simple, wore arms), and asked him if he
could direct her on the way to the Castle of
Greenan.

"And what may ye want at Greenan, my
guid woman? I mysel' live close by the
Castle, and if ye'll tak' a friend's advice ye'll
stay in the toun; for if Lord Kennedy happens
to be at hame—which, nevertheless, is hardly
likely—he'll set his dogs on ye."

Still the poor woman pleaded to be informed
of the whereabouts of Greenan, and at last
the kindly-hearted countryman said he "wud
gie her a lift as far as Greenan on his forage

cairt," which he soon accordingly did, and
ere the evening was far advanced the strolling
musician was thrumming her lute in the
frowning courtyard of Greenan Castle.

Poor wretch! It was indeed a sad sight
to see her, who ought to have herself been
receiving creature comforts, making gasping
efforts to comfort others by the sound of voice
and lute. Alas, alas! the case is too common.
As a rule those most in want of comfort are
those who receive least.

With a voice of much plaintive sweetness the minstrel soon afterwards sang as
follows :—

> " There is an hour of peaceful rest
>   To mourning wanderers given:
> There is a tear for souls distrest,
> A balm for every wounded breast;
>   'Tis found above—in heaven.

> " There is a soft and downy bed,
>   'Tis fair as breath of even:
> A couch for weary mortals spread,
> Where they may rest the aching head,
>   And find repose—in heaven.

" There is a home for weeping souls,
  By sin and sorrow driven;
When toss'd on life's tempestuous shoals,
Where storms arise, and ocean rolls,
  And all is drear—but heaven.

" There fragrant flowers immortal bloom,
  And joys supreme are given;
There rays divine disperse the gloom;
Beyond the confines of the tomb
  Appears the dawn—of heaven! "

But the effort was evidently too much for
the exhausted strolling minstrel. Had it not
been for the kindly care of some of the Castle
domestics she would have fallen fainting to
the ground. Soon, however, she was assisted
inside, and Lady Kennedy gave orders that
she should be assiduously attended to. But
such attention seemed to be of little avail;
the poor creature rapidly got worse. The
hand of death was plainly upon her, as she
solemnly said, " In God I put my trust."
At last she asked, in piteous accents, to see a
priest.

" A priest, did ye say?" exclaimed the

old female servant in attendance; "a priest, did ye say? Na, na, my poor woman, ye'll find nae priests here. Thank guidness, when the monastic rookeries were pu'd doun, the priestly rooks quickly flew awa'. And a guid thing, tae."

The statement that there was no priest in the locality was really not true. In a cottage just behind the brow of the hill, and overlooking the sea, there had long dwelt Father Garthwaite. He had now no chapel, and but few followers, as it had become dangerous to be known as a papist; but the priest, it was well enough understood, received very considerable, although strictly private, support from Lady Kennedy, and with the sanction of her husband, if not indeed by his direct orders.

"Then I must see Lady Kennedy," said the dying woman.

"Must!" retorted the other earnestly but not unkindly; "ye mauna 'must' here. The leddy may come and see you, as she generally sees onybody in distress; but nane o' your

Popish mummeries wi' her. No that," she quietly added aside, "she hasna still a hankerin' after them; nor his Lordship either."

Say not, kind reader, that the poor stroller was doing wrong in asking for a dispenser of the ghostly consolation and absolution peculiar to those of her faith. Surely, even from Protestant Scotland a devout Roman Catholic is likely to receive as much favour on the Great Day as will a devout Protestant Presbyterian. "Judge not, that ye be not judged."

Lady Kennedy soon appeared on the sad scene. She was a tall, wan, commandingly beautiful woman, evidently much younger than she looked; her dark hair was considerably streaked with grey before she was even thirty years of age.

The strolling musician asked to be left alone with my lady, and her request having been complied with—although not without some degree of reluctance on the part of the old domestic—she raised herself in the bed, and in a voice hollow with exhaustion and emotion, began,—

"Lady Kennedy, listen ! A little more than seven years ago my real name was Marie Stuart de Guise, and I believe I am a direct descendent of the family to which belonged the unfortunate Mary Queen of Scots. I was a novitiate in the Convent de Sulpice, in Paris. Circumstances, which I need not here detail, brought me into the society of a handsome young Scotch nobleman who was then being educated in that city. After paying his addresses to me, and after my foolishly, as I now think, listening to them, we were privately married by a Carmelite monk."

Here the poor stroller fell back on the bed, panting for dear breath.

"My peculiar condition having in time been discovered, to save both our lives we were forced to flee, my husband to Scotland, and I to Bordeaux, where ultimately I was delivered of a female child."

Once more the dying woman paused, and

bitter tears traced themselves down her wan cheeks. After a few further gasps she continued—

"The Lady Superior of the Convent de Sulpice having discovered my whereabouts, I was, along with my child, placed in confinement, and a communication was sent to my husband that I was dead. However, it was not long ere I escaped, and got a passage to this country on board a wine-ship, which was wrecked not far from here. Believing that the boat in which some of the crew and myself had taken voyage before the ship was dashed to pieces would also be lost—(but it was not, thank God!)—I, with the assistance of a kind sailor, tied my babe to an oar, and launched it, near the shore, on the troubled waters. Ultimately we were saved, but where, oh where, was my child?"

Another anxious pause, and during this pause both women—lady as well as lute-player—wept copiously.

"Through the instrumentality of a discharged valet of my husband, whom I met

by accident, I found that my child was in
Glasgow, and God only knows how I have
toiled, as a teacher of music, to feed, clothe,
and educate her."

" You will receive your reward in heaven,"
said Lady Kennedy, tenderly.

Again Marie Stuart de Guise went on :—
" Finding that my strength was failing fast,
and that my poor Gabrielle—named after my
own sainted mother—was likely after my
death to be an outcast on the world "—and
now the speaker painfully shuddered—" a
week ago I bought a lute, determined, from
what I had heard of your ladyship's goodness, to beg my way until I found you.
At last, *remercie mon Dieu!* that wish has
been gratified, but I shall never more behold
my Gabrielle.   Now, lady, my last, my
dying request is, Will you see to the future
of my poor child ?"

"The name of your lost husband?" earnestly
and tearfully asked the now astonished Lady
Kennedy.

" This sealed packet," she answered, as

she handed Lady Kennedy what she alleged was a marriage certificate, "will inform you, but it must not be opened until I am gone. I freely forgive *him;* but will you, my good lady, care for my beloved child, my sweet Gabrielle? She will never, I feel more than assured, disgrace thy kind patronage, nor bring a tear of sorrow or shame into thy loving eyes. Speak, lady, speak! it will soon be too late!"

Just one brief pause, and then, "Your request is granted," was sobbed by the lady. This was followed by "Now, Lord, let Thy servant depart in peace," from the dying woman. In a few minutes she repeated the Latin prayer written by the unfortunate Queen Mary before her execution by Elizabeth:—

"O Domine Jesu, speravi in Te,
 O care mi Jesu, nunc libera me;
   In durâ catenâ,
   In miserâ pœnâ,
     Desidero Te;
 Languendo, dolendo, et genu flectendo,
 Adoro, imploro, ut liberes me."

Which may be freely translated into English
in the following words :—

> "O my God and my Lord, I have trusted in Thee,
> O Jesus, my love, now liberate me ;
>   In Death's mighty power,
>   In affliction's sad hour,
>   I languish for Thee.
> In sorrowing, weeping, and bending the knee,
> I adore and implore Thee to liberate me."

Then the poor but now happy mother
kissed a little silver crucifix, and asked permission to embrace Lady Kennedy. This
permission was readily granted by the kindly-
hearted lady, who in turn kissed her tenderly,
and shed not a few tears on the face of the
unfortunate Marie.

"Weep not for me, kind lady. *En
Dieu est ma fiance*," she said, and quietly
died.

Yes, she was dead; but not dead in tres-
passes and sin. Nay, but the very opposite
—in holiness and happiness. The poor
Roman Catholic strolling-player's soul was
set free. She died, too, in the sure hope of

a blessed resurrection. "Blessed are the dead who die in the Lord."

And the noble lady of Greenan Castle knelt at the bedside of the dead, and prayed that she too might, in God's good time, be as able and willing to depart in peace from this sorrowful earth to the happiness of the Silent Land.

.   .   .   .

Next morning it was noticed by the domestics that Lady Kennedy's hair was much lighter in hue than it had ever been before; while a settled gloom had taken firm possession of her marble-looking countenance.

CHAPTER IV.

OLD GLASGOW.

"An extensive and increasing traffic with the West
  Indies and American Colonies has, if I am rightly
  informed, laid in Glasgow the foundation of
  wealth and industry, which, if carefully strength-
  ened and built upon, may one day support an
  immense fabric of commercial prosperity."—*Sir
  Walter Scott (1817).*

CITY of Saint Mungo, may thy shadow
never grow less!—may thy hospitable
inhabitants ever go on increasing in prosperity
and wealth! Long may thy noble river send
forth to the very ends of the earth ships
unsurpassed for strength and unrivalled for
speed!

Thou hast, noble city, in remarkably short
space, raised thyself to the proud position of
Second City in the Empire.

At the time, however, of which we write,
Glasgow was not the Second City; in fact,

not long before that period Glasgow only ranked in importance about ninth or tenth among the towns of Scotland. It is true it long previously had its grand Cathedral and its great University; but progress in theology is a very slow thing when compared with progress in commerce. Strangely enough, men are inclined to make money first, leaving their eternal welfare until later on in life, when they think they will have more time to look after eternity!

But our present business is not to moralise. In a few days after the death of the unfortunate Marie Stuart de Guise, her remains were unostentatiously interred in the pretty little kirk-yard of Alloway, a place that has since been immortalised in Burns's "Tam o' Shanter."

The somewhat strange and sorrowful events that had so suddenly occurred were as yet unknown to Lord Kennedy, who had been absent during the time of their occurrence. And it was very unlikely he would take any interest in the matters even when informed

of them.   His Lordship was too much engaged
in wars and rumours of wars to attend to
domestic matters, or even to matters directly
connected with the conduct of his extensive
estates.

Mr Godfrey Marling was the factor at
Greenan, and occupied the home farm of
Greyscaur.   He was an Englishman, who had
been successful in cattle breeding and sheep
farming, and had long been engaged by Lord
Kennedy for the purpose of improving the
very backward state of agriculture that
existed at Greenan.

Mr Marling had one day suddenly been
sent for by Lady Kennedy, and received a
certain commission to execute ; and on a
bright afternoon in August he all at once
turned up in the city of Glasgow.   The day
was very hot, and, as Mr Marling was
corpulent, he stopped every now and again
to wipe the streaming perspiration from his
manly brow.   He had ridden full forty miles,
and he now thought it would have been better
not to have put up his horse at a hostelry

until he had found the address of which he was at present in such hot search.

But Mr Marling was a merciful man, and the merciful man is merciful to his beast.

Glasgow, it may not be generally known, is not unfrequently a very hot place in summer. Occasionally, in fact, the meteorological returns show that some Glasgow and Edinburgh summers are hotter than even those of London and Paris. And at the time of Mr Marling's visit the streets of St Mungo were not nearly so broad nor so well kept as they are now. They were, in fact, of the narrowest that can be possibly imagined, and well merited the description that Burns long afterwards gave of the Auld Brig of Ayr :—

> " Puir narrow footpath o' a street,
> Where twa wheelbarrows tremble when they meet."

Mr Marling walked about—almost without a trace of the energy which he was known usually to possess—in the most intricate part of Glasgow, where streets tortuously crossed each other in every direction; and it was not surprising that a stranger should lose himself, as Mr Marling did, in the annoying maze of turnings and windings.

Mr Marling had received strict injunctions that his mission was of a secret character, and as he was always faithful to his trust he had determined not to ask his way of anyone, and was just about, for that afternoon, to give up the search, when all at once he became pleasantly aware that he was not only in the very street, but opposite the very house for which he was searching; and, to the astonishment of a number of barefooted and mostly bareheaded boys, Mr Marling suddenly shouted "Eureka!"

The appearance of the house was, like the neighbourhood, far from promising. There was, to put it very mildly, an evident want of sanitary arrangements about the whole place. The water supply was not then from St Katrine's Loch. In fact, there did not seem to be any water supply at all. If there were, it did not appear to be made use of by the inhabitants either on themselves or on their dwellings.

But Mr Marling was not a man to be daunted by appearances, which he well knew were often deceitful. Accordingly, he went to the door of the house wanted, and knocked loudly. But he received no response. Again he knocked, and still more loudly, with a similar absence of result. At last he kicked at the door, and with some effect, for a window was raised, and the shrill voice of a woman shouted—

" And what may ye want ? "

" Admission," was Mr Marling's curt and pointed reply.

" Gang awa' wi' ye ; ye'll get nae admission here, I tell ye."

" But, my good woman, I have important business to transact with you."

" Dinna ' guid woman' me, my guid man. Gin ye dinna at aince leave my door, I'll may be gi'e ye sich a droukin' that'll let ye ken whether I'm a guid woman or no ; and that just as sure's my name's Macnish ! "

Mr Marling was non-plussed—even flab-bergasted, to use a too common vulgarism.

He had nothing to say. Then Mrs Macnish, getting a little refreshed at her intending visitor's silence, returned to the encounter.

"Ye lang ago," she continued, while her wrath rapidly rose; "ye lang ago filled my ain man fou, 'listed him, and killed him dead in the wars. Then ye cam' wi' yer infernal press-gang, and took awa' my bonnie son. Noo, I suppose, ye want to tak' *me* awa!

"God forbid!" involuntarily ejaculated Mr Marling. And then apologetically he said, "I wish, Mrs Macnish, to speak with you concerning a little girl under your care."

"An' what for did ye no say that before?" she asked, as she sulkily closed the window, and came slowly down stairs.

Mr Marling soon afterwards got admittance, and while Mrs Macnish led the way to an inner apartment, she grumbled out her grievances after the most loquacious and garrulous Scotch fashion. Her husband, she said—and a guid husband he was when out o' the drink —had been one of the best journeymen curriers

in the ceety o' Glasgow. He had for years
plied his calling in Paris, where he had learnt
to be more efficient than most Scotchmen,
aye, and even than most frog-eating Frenchmen; &c., &c.

Then she led Mr Marling into a decent-
sized room that betokened poverty, but
showed that strict cleanliness prevailed in the
domicile of the Macnishes.

"But wha may ye be, and what dae ye
want wi' the lassie, and whaur's her mither?"
were questions Mrs Macnish put in quick and
continuous succession. "Ye may be a guid
aneuch man, for ye look sonsy, but my mither
aye said that like was an ill mark. Ye're no'
a Scotchman—I ken by yer tongue—and, by
the same token, ye're no' a Frenchman. Ye
appear to me to be a pock-puddin', beef-
devourin' Englishman—deil tak' their big
bellies!"

"Never mind my nationality," said Mr
Marling; "I have come here to be of good
service to the girl Gabrielle, and possibly to
yourself. I wish to take her away."

"Ah, weel; but ye maun see her mither first and foremost."

"I am afraid, Mrs Macnish, that none of us will ever see the child's mother on this side of the grave."

"So muckle the mair reason, then," said Mrs Macnish, with a tear in her eye, "that I should look after the lassie. I can keep mysel' by lace-knitting, and the bairn will soon be able to do the same for hersel'."

Mr Marling, then, as tenderly as he could, explained the manner of the death of poor Marie, and told Mrs Macnish that Lady Kennedy had undertaken to provide for the child.

"And I have no doubt," he added, "that if you choose to accompany the girl, the good lady will also provide for you."

"But hoo am I tae ken that a' this ye're tellin' me is true or no?" pertinently asked the cautious Scotchwomen.

"By this same token," answered Mr Marling; and he held up the silver crucifix that the unfortunate Marie had so fervently kissed while on her death-bed.

Then Mrs Macnish fell into a fearful paroxysm of grief.

"God knows," she sobbed, "if ever there was an angel on earth it was that bairn's mither. And what'll the poor wean say or dae when she hears the awfu' news? Heaven help her in this sad affliction!"

Mr Marling did his best to assuage the sorrow of the good woman, and soon she was prevailed upon to bring young Gabrielle into the apartment. Mr Marling was indeed surprised when she entered. He was a great admirer of female loveliness; but in all his experience—and it was extensive—he had never seen a girl so beautiful.

With an intelligent face, and an air of entire self-possession, she was, in her neat black dress, a charming little picture. As she entered, Gabrielle curtseyed somewhat coldly to Mr Marling; but, on being reassured by Dame Macnish, she took his extended hand.

Mr Marling then lifted her in his arms, and placed her lovingly on his knee—a

proceeding which Gabrielle resented, first
with a look of indignation, and then by
saying, " You might have asked my permission before you took such a liberty."

Mr Marling was both astonished and
amused at this, and as he began, " I am
really very very sorry——"

But he was interrupted by little Gabrielle
with " Well, if you are really sorry, let us
say no more about it, as I wish to hear from
my good, kind mother.   I presume you come
with a message from her ? "

The cloud that passed over Mr Marling's
brow, and the tears that had sadly reddened
Mrs Macnish's eyes, were at once noticed by
the quick and observant Gabrielle.

" Where is my mother ? " she tearfully
exclaimed, as she fell on her knees at Mr
Marling's feet.   " Why, oh why, does she
not come back to me ?   Tell me, kind sir,
tell me."

It was now Mr Marling's time to weep.
But he soon dashed away his unaccustomed
tears.   After a few moments had elapsed he

said, as tenderly as a woman could have
said,—

· "Your good mother, my dear little Gabrielle, has gone to that land where there is
no sorrow, for there God wipes away all
tears."

The grief of Gabrielle, who in a moment
saw the terrible position in which she was
placed, was of the most poignant character.
So great was it that for a time the good
landlady and Mr Marling were afraid the
child would lose her reason.

She was carried to bed, and the kind-
hearted Scotchwoman tended the child most
affectionately until she fell asleep. Next
day Mr Marling returned, and found Gabrielle
still prostrate from the effects of the sudden
shock the intelligence of the death of her
mother had produced.

In a day or two, however, Gabrielle's grief
was toned down by the kind consolations
of her two seniors, and arrangements were
quietly made for their speedy departure from
Glasgow. Mr Marling paid Mrs Macnish's

house rent up to the end of her current year, and the house was duly locked up. For her absent son, in the event of his return, the good woman left her Greenan address with her husband's late employer; and one bright, sunny morning saw Gabrielle and her two sage friends leave Glasgow for the purpose of proceeding further west—that is, they went in the direction of Auld Ayr.

That the still sorrowing child might not be too much fatigued, a halt was made that night at Kilmarnock, then little more than a village, but celebrated for its manufacture of broad blue bonnets and "cowls," or night-caps, which latter, however, were almost as much worn during the day as during the night. The following afternoon the little Gabrielle found herself safely at the Home Farm of Greenan (where, of course, she never knew she had been before), under the care of Mrs Marling, as good and as kind a woman as ever baked a bannock or made a haggis.

CHAPTER V.

WONDERING.

" Now the plantin' taps are tinged wi' gowd
On yon burn side,
And gloamin' draws her foggy shroud
O'er yon burn side ;
Far frae the noisy scene,
I'll through the fields alane :
There we'll meet my ain dear Jean !
Doun by yon burn side."

Tannahill.

" What may this mean, that thou, dread corse,
Revisitest thus the glimpses of the moon,
Making night hideous ? "

Shakespeare.

TANNAHILL ! Among the best, but, in my humble opinion, the most neglected, of Scottish poets. Paisley has abounded, perhaps, above all other Scotch towns, in poets. Alas for Robert Tannahill, the greatest of them all ! Next to Burns, no Scottish song-writer has exercised so much

influence over the minds of the song-singing
community of Scotland; and it is questionable
if even Robert Burns, as a mere song-writer,
was, in that particular poetical sphere, greater
than Robert Tannahill. Now we sing Tannahill's songs, but we seldom mention his name.
But let us trust that Tannahill's name and
fame will yet be resounded throughout
Scotland.

Tannahill touched the tender strings of the
musical harp as few other song-writers ever
did; but he strung the strings of his harp
too tightly. Tannahill's bright "Lass of
Arranteenie" gave way at times to such
strains as the solemn but glorious "Despair-
ing Mary." The strings of his harp were, we
repeat, far too tightly strung. The best
string, the "mind" string, suddenly snapped,
and Robert Tannahill one day made a death-
plunge in a little pool near Paisley that is
still called "Tannahill's Hole." Heaven help
us!

Still, the unfortunate end of a great man
is not to be considered a sufficient reason

why his memory should be neglected. Hugh Miller sought his own end quite as unfortunately as did Robert Tannahill. Join their memories, then, together. In each case the diseased mind got the better of the frail man. But while we remember Miller, let us not forget Tannahill. Why should Scotland, in a metaphorical manner, adopt the dreadful verdict of *Felo de se*, that disgraces the law of inquest in England?

The only excuses I can make for this digression regarding Tannahill are, first, that his songs have ever appeared to me to be peculiarly and plaintively sweet; and next, that the exquisite quotation I have made at the head of this chapter from his "Doun by Yon Burnside" well suits the working out of some of the details of our present chapter.

. . . . .

One lovely harvest evening, after the sun had sunk behind Arran hills, and for a time given the Great Goatfell a golden hue, a young man, evidently belonging to the superior agricultural class, was sauntering along from Greyscaur towards a tall tryst-ing-tree which spread its birken branches across a whimpling burn that contributed its quota to the murmuring waters of the gentle Doon, now so celebrated in immortal song by our national bard.

This burn, it appears—and it can still be seen by the inquiring tourist—is the only stream in Scotland that runs away from the sea! According to common report, the burn changed its course on a particular night when Lord Kennedy roasted a Bishop at the Lady Isle. But it appears to me that the stream merely seems, by an easily explained optical illusion, to be running away from the sea. By a little tortuous meandering it ultimately finds its way into the Doon, and necessarily to the sea.

The young man, Guy Gordon, was hum-ming a tune, the words of which, from the occasional snatches that he gave boldly forth, were not unlike those of a very favourite Scotch song not then written or even thought of:—

" Come a' ye jolly shepherds
   That whistle through the glen,
I'll tell ye o' a secret
   That courtiers dinna ken ;
What is the greatest bliss
   That the tongue o' man can name ?
'Tis to woo a bonnie lassie
   When the kye comes hame."

In the present case the Greenan kye had come hame, the ewes were in the fauld, and the lambs were lying still. The gowden tinge on the plantin' taps had given way to the foggy shroud o' gloamin', and the harvest moon was rising in all her glory through the silvery lift. It was indeed a lovely night.

All that was wanting to complete the picture was the bonnie lassie. And it was not long ere she made her appearance. A comely quean she was, too. Her flaxen hair was neatly done up in the " snood " that was wont to be worn by Scottish maidens, and is still worn by unmarried females in some parts of France. Neat bodice covered a well-developed bust, while a crimson kirtle was sufficiently curtailed to show a foot and ankle that, even in the moonlight, might have been envied by a princess.

Jean Graham—for such was the name of the pretty damsel—was my lady's maid—or tiring-woman, as it was then expressed—and she had come to keep tryst with her betrothed, Guy Gordon, who was at once my lord's forester, falconer, and deerstalker—positions of trust and importance that Guy, strangely enough, continually contemned.

Almost from his boyhood Guy had had a grievance. He was never taken with his lord and master on any warlike expedition. And Guy loved fighting. He had boxed and fenced, and conquered all-comers in the parish, and he would certainly have been a valuable adjunct to any war party. But Lord Kennedy had found Guy Gordon such a useful fellow on the estate that he kept him continually there. In this way many a man of ability has his success in life retarded because he happens to fit the humble sphere in which he at the particular time is placed.

At the Malt Cross of Ayr, on gallivanting

days, and even in Glasgow on the occasion
of high festivals, and they were frequent,
Guy Gordon always kept the crown o' the
causeway ; while in the Laigh Green who but
Guy was the best archer, the best wrestler,
and the best breaker of a head with a quarter-
staff ?　And who but Guy—and oft this gave
Jean Graham a terrible heart-pang—was the
most favoured by the bonnie lasses of Auld
Ayr ?

The Magistrates—jolly fellows, who loved
the feast and the flowing bowl—had inaug-
urated horse-racing, and Guy Gordon had
actually won three out of the five events in a
recent day's racing programme.

Guy affectionately saluted his true love
with a hearty kiss as she reached the well-
known trysting-tree.

"Save my snood, rude fellow, save my
snood ! Think you I am made of as rough
material as the web-footed woman with
whom you were so familiar in the town the
other night ? "

Guy now looked utterly astonished as he

exclaimed, "How on earth do you get all the news?"

"Just as murder will out so will faithlessness," said Jean Graham, and she stamped her handsome little foot with puny rage.

"But, dearest, on the cross of my sword, on my honour as a man, on my faith as a Christian, on my——"

"Swear not at all," interrupted the incensed maiden; "the Recording Angel alone knows how many false oaths are daily recorded in the Book of Fate."

"Well, let me explain. The poor woman had been nearly drowned in fording the river from Newton, and, being a Roman Catholic, she had knelt at the old cross in High Street, and was uttering her thanks to Heaven, when a number of the boys of the Black Gang attacked her, crying, 'Out upon the Papist hag! To the Malt Cross with her, and let her have a touch of tar and a few feathers!' And they would have executed their infernal intent had I not cracked a few of their crowns, and hurried the poor thing off to her destination in the Townhead."

The Black Gang was an organised band of young fellows, whose origin was for the purpose of ridding the town of pests, but they themselves soon became greater pests than even the pests had been.

"But what about the very fond embrace when you parted?" And still the maiden's anger rose.

"Nay, love, you wrong me. The affrighted creature did but ask to kiss the hand of her deliverer, and I told her she might kiss him where she chose, when she put her pale lips gently to my cheek."

"And you have the confidence, the impudence, to place your polluted cheek against mine! Methinks it was asking heavy largess for small services when the brazen hussy made such a bold and unwomanly request."

"But the chances are I saved her life. Yet I humbly ask your forgiveness."

"Well, well let it end; but I tell you, I

much dislike this Papistical lot; more than
ever, too, since this wonderful little Gabrielle
has come so strangely and suddenly amongst
us; for day after day I take her to the
cottage of Father Garthwaite and return for
her at the end of two hours. Sometimes she
forgets to hide her crucifix, an emblem I
abhor. I feel assured she is being brought
up as a horrid Roman."

"And what about it?" asked Guy. "Is
not a good Roman Catholic as good as a
good Presbyterian?"

"No, no, she isn't. Besides, Gabrielle and
Mr Garthwaite always talk in French. I
know it is French, because it has the same
sound as has the language of the French
sailors who come into the Port of Ayr.
There can be no doubt about that crucifix
meaning Popery, and Popery means per-
secution."

"Fie, fie, love! The emblem of our
redemption ought to be as sacred in the
eyes of the Protestant as the Roman
Catholic. As for the little girl, I already

love her so much that I think I could lay
down my life for her."

"Pshaw! You are always talking about
laying down your life; in a brawl, some fine
day, you'll do it really."

"Well, my love, my father, who had some
of the best blood of Scotland in his veins,
was a soldier, and why may I not follow Lord
Kennedy, as my sire did his?"

"And much he made of it, my dear Sir
Grievance Guy, seeing that your father was
slain. Whereas, had he continued to be
forester and factor here, he might have been
a help and a comfort to your now aged
mother. But to return, Sir Guy; What
think you of this little star Gabrielle, that
has all at once appeared on the Greenan
firmament? Who is she? whence came she?
and what will my lord say when he returns?"

"I trouble myself nought about these
things," replied Guy indifferently; "I suppose
my lord will treat the matter with his usual
coldness and apathy. All I know about the
little lady is that, for her years, she is the

most accomplished child I ever met. She is, in fact, what strolling mummers call an infant prodigy."

"But you know that the breath of scandal is already being breathed about the little girl, whom I must confess I like very much; although," she added archly, "I would not altogether like to lay down my life for her. Still, everybody is wondering."

"Let them all wonder as much as they choose," said Guy; "they are always wondering about something."

"Then they refer to the night when a child was rescued at Lady Isle, and the sudden illness of Lord Kennedy, who has never been the same man since. Besides, the coincidence of the death of the foreign musician, and the almost immediate appearance of Miss Gabrielle Stuart, is strongly commented on."

"Never mind, love; never mind," said Guy, "I have something else to talk to thee about. I wish to arrange for our going to the forthcoming festival at Glasgow. There is to be a two days' tourney and innumerable sports."

"Ah, but," she continued, scarcely heeding the interruption, "it was a fearful night that on which the foreign woman died. My lady, after returning to her own room, began to peruse certain papers which she had evidently received from the wretched person. She had not been long so engaged when she gave a loud scream of pain, and when I entered I found her deadly pale. 'It is nothing,' she said, 'I wish to be alone;' and I retired. But my lady herself never retired to rest during all that long night."

"Well," said Guy, "that is no uncommon thing with Lady Kennedy."

"But listen, Guy. At the usual hour in the morning I quietly entered her chamber and found her kneeling in front of that same crucifix now worn by Gabrielle. Lady Kennedy was so absorbed in her devotions that she did not observe my entrance. I heard her pray, 'Holy Virgin, intercede for me; I know that I have merited all my punishment, but, Blessed Lady, it is greater than I can bear!'"

"I am indeed sorry for the unhappy lady," said Guy; "but what could she mean by saying that she merited all her punishment? And wherein consists the punishment?"

"Hush!" said his lover, looking timorously round, "there is some terrible meaning under it. God grant that it may not be anything like so sad as I suppose."

"Amen," responded Guy.

"I hastily retired," once more continued Jean Graham, "and when I was called some time afterwards I found that in one night there had been upwards of ten years added to my lady's age, and that her hair had turned nearly white."

"It is indeed a painful state of matters. My lord is much to blame."

"Much to blame!" said Jean, excitedly: "much to blame! Why, he is not even fit to live. Only to-day I overheard Mr Marling tell his wife that my lord was at present cohabiting with another of his concubines in Edinburgh. And you have heard of the dreadful story of his former *liason* in that city. Only think of the poor neglected Magdalene being suddenly ushered into the presence of her Maker, with all her sins upon her head."

"But Jean, the wretched woman was confessed, and had the last rites of the holy Church administered to her."

"Confessed!" exclaimed Jean with indignation; "Confessed! And what, pray, is confession to frail man? The last rites of the holy Church cannot keep the spirit of the murdered woman at rest, for I am told that it still, at certain times, is to be seen in this very neighbourhood."

"Nay, not a word more of that tragical affair," interpolated Guy.

"And the poor, innocent, unbaptised infant, too. Oh, it's fate is too terrible even to contemplate!" And the pretty maiden wept bitterly.

"Come, dearest, dry thy tears; thou canst not improve matters."

"But I feel they ought to be improved, and I am certain that some fearful retribution will ensue. Sin, I firmly believe, is punished here as well as hereafter."

"Nay, love, thou must not speculate in such unusual fashion. The Almighty works in His own all-wise way."

Talking thus, the lovers wandered by the side of the placid Doon until the silvery moon was getting high in the starry heavens.

Returning towards the Castle, they passed close to Father Garthwaite's cottage, and were startled to hear the sweet strains of an organ accompanying a trained choir singing the glorious "Kyrie Eleison."

It was evident there was a considerable company gathered within, and that the interior of the house was brilliantly lighted.

"An organ and a choir in Father Garthwaite's cottage!" exclaimed Jean Graham, in astonishment.

"Yes, it does, indeed, seem passing strange," responded Guy.

" More Papacy, more Papacy ! What is all this to end in ? See, see ! a hare has just crossed our path. I feel assured something dreadful is about to happen soon."

This was the common superstition of the time, as I suppose it is now.

Suddenly the music ceased, and the light in the priest's cottage as suddenly disappeared.

" Gracious heavens ! " ejaculated Jean, " I had forgotten that this is the anniversary of the terrible night. And there, of a certainty, comes the Weeping Lady ! "

Even the usually brave Guy Gordon stood as if he were transfixed, and with mingled astonishment and awe depicted on his manly countenance.

There, wandering distractedly by the side of the river, and peering into every nook and cranny, was the figure of a lady in white. Wringing her hands convulsively, and weeping piteously, the wretched being continually wailed—

"Where's my bairn, my bonnie bairn, my murdered bairn?"

The Weeping Lady seemed to be surpassingly beautiful, but her face was as ashy pale as that of a corpse. She seemed to glide rather than walk by the river's bank.

"God save us from this uncanny being!" exclaimed the frightened girl.

"Never fear," said Guy, "she seems harmless enough, poor thing."

As the figure passed closely by the lovers without in any way noticing them, Jean swooned in the arms of Guy Gordon.

Slowly the Weeping Lady disappeared round a bend in the dark river, but still the young man could distinctly hear the wailing sound—

"Where's my bairn, my bonnie bairn, my murdered bairn?"

Guy was in a sad plight with the insensible maiden. He ran to the river, from which he brought water in his bonnet, and bathed her throbbing temples.

Soon Jean recovered sufficiently to walk

from the place.   Yet still, as the lovers
neared the Castle, they could plainly hear
the pitiful wail—

"Where's my bairn, my bonnie bairn, my
murdered bairn?"

CHAPTER VI.

GABRIELLE.

" This lovely creature of herself
Is all-sufficient. Solitude to her
Is blythe society, who fills the air
With gladness and involuntary songs.
Light are her sallies as the tripping fawn's.
Forth startled from the fern where she lay couch'd."

Wordsworth.

AUTUMN had waned into winter, and winter had naturally been followed by spring. Gabrielle still pursued her studies under the care of Father Garthwaite, who was generally materially assisted by Lady Kennedy.

Lord Kennedy had returned to Greenan Castle, after an unusually prolonged absence. One day, my Lady coldly told him the sad story of the strolling musician, carefully omitting all mention of the sealed packet. My Lord as coldly listened to the tale, and

silently consented to the adoption of
Gabrielle, who was sent for to be introduced
to his Lordship. She came, and Lord
Kennedy gave a start of surprise when he
saw her.

"So you are the child of the poor woman
who died suddenly in this Castle ?"

"My Lord," answered Gabrielle, "I am.
But I have always been accustomed to hear
my mother talked of as a lady."

At once a mutual dislike sprung up
between the two. Deny it who so list,
men and women are prone to have their
likes and their dislikes, without being able
to account for them. It is said he is a bad
man who dislikes dogs or children ; but the
statement is as stupid as it is untruthful.
Most men like their own children, and dislike comparatively those of others ; while not
a few good men have an utter and life-long
abhorrence of dogs.

It was arranged that Gabrielle should come
to the Castle daily, that Lady Kennedy
should visit her as frequently as she chose,

but that in the meantime the girl's regular residence was to be at Greyscaur.

Then my Lord, after bowing stiffly, retired to an inner apartment, there to study new schemes of vengeance on the Crafty Crawfords. He was meditating a plan of either attack or defence, for his numerous retainers and allies had been for several nights mysteriously entering the Castle grounds, as if making ready for or expecting a raid to be made upon them.

.   .   .   .   .

Lady Kennedy and Gabrielle, shortly after the interview, were slowly sauntering towards the Home Farm. For a time they spoke not, each being seriously absorbed in her own reflections. At last Gabrielle broke the silence.

"Pardon me, my good Lady. The other day you were kind enough to say that you thought you would soon be able to let me know something of my parents. May I be bold enough, now that Lord Kennedy has returned, to ask if you can carry out the promise?"

Lady Kennedy pressed her hand on her heart as if in great pain.

"Nay, my Lady," said Gabrielle, "think me not rude. I am sorry indeed if I have annoyed you or caused you the slightest pain."

"It is nothing, my dear Gabrielle, but a passing pang. As to your question, I have only to say that to-day I have changed my mind as to the time when I may give you some account of your parents. Believe me, it will be as soon as it can conveniently be done."

"Thanks, my good Lady," said Gabrielle; but a tear rose involuntarily to her eye.

Another lengthened silence ensued, and when the outer grounds of Greyscaur were reached, Lady Kennedy affectionately embraced Gabrielle, and returned towards the Castle; while Gabrielle made a detour, and took a solitary stroll in the neighbouring wood.

That night, or rather early in the following

morning, a "horrid whisper" fell on the
Home Farm. Guy Gordon, in returning
late from the town, found to his dismay
that the Castle had been secretly invested
by the Crawfords and other enemies of the
Kennedys, and that they were waiting for
the break of day, when they meant to
storm the place.

Mr Marling and all the inmates of his
house were soon astir. What was to be
done? It was impossible to alarm the
Castle. The situation was perilous in the
extreme, and old Marling and Guy Gordon
were almost beside themselves with anxiety
as to the prospective fate of their friends.
Greyscaur could only muster six men, all
told, and what were they to at least
three hundred of the enemy. To venture
outside the Home Farm meant to be put
to violent death by the besiegers, without being of the slightest benefit to the
besieged.

Gabrielle grasped the situation at once,
and gently said, " Wrap an old plaid around

me, and give me my dear mother's lute. I
unhesitatingly undertake—in fact, I consider
it is my duty—to give the alarm at the
Castle."

"You, child!" exclaimed Mr Marling;
"get you to my wife's bedroom, and do not
be afraid. God will protect us."

"Afraid!" she exclaimed, while the blood
mounted to her young cheeks. Then, re-
suming her former gentle tone, she said—

"I well know the little bedroom window
of Miss Graham, my lady's tire-woman, and
I can give her the alarm."

"Why, my dear child, that little window
is in the strong tower that faces the sea, and
is quite inaccessible."

"At anyrate, I'll try," said Gabrielle, with
a fixed determination that seemed far beyond
her sex and much above her years. And she
quickly made preparations for proceeding
on her dangerous mission.

"Godspeed the child!" was the exclamation from every lip as the heroic girl,
commending herself to the Virgin, walked

out into the black night. Guy Gordon
attempted to follow Gabrielle, but Mr Marling forcibly restrained him. And Mr
Marling was right. It was desirable that
the utmost caution should be observed where
so many of their friends' lives were involved,
not to consider the loss of the Castle itself
and the adjacent estate.

The little window to which Gabrielle had
referred did indeed face the ocean, and might
fairly be called inaccessible. The sea had
washed away the small portion of land that
had once been in front of the donjon-keep of
the Castle, and left a mere ridge of turf
showing where the ground had once been.
Some of the more adventurous of the boys
about Greenan had been in the habit of
boldly venturing along that frail ridge, but
one poor little fellow, not long before,
had lost his footing, and was dashed to
pieces on the rugged rocks below. In consequence of this dreadful disaster, a wooden
balustrade had been erected at the side of
the tower, and strict orders given that no

one was ever again to attempt the dangerous passage.*

Gabrielle passed quietly through the wood, or plantin' as it is more commonly called in Scotland, and soon came upon the beaten round of a sentinel; but her light footstep was unheard by the half-sleepy man-at-arms. Turning to the left, and keeping as close as possible to the shore, Gabrielle was not long in reaching the exposed side of the " keep."

Fortunately the night was unusually dark, and through the darkness Gabrielle could not sufficiently appreciate the terrible danger she was about to incur.

Laying her lute on the ground she nimbly scrambled over the balustrade, and fearlessly but cautiously set foot on the dangerous ridge.

---

* There is no exaggeration in the description here given. In his youth the present writer was more than once foolhardy enough to venture along the frail ridge; and it is not many years since a boy was dashed to pieces in attempting to cross the dangerous pass.

Deep down below the waves thundered angrily against the rocks; but Gabrielle looked not beneath. Clinging closely to the rough wall, in less than a minute she reached the little stanchioned window, and began to knock. But there was no attention paid to the sounds she made. Louder and louder she knocked, until her little knuckles were sorely abrazed.

At last Jean Graham, who had been enjoying the female consolation of a good cry, because Guy Gordon had not met her in the evening at the trysting-tree—"Men were deceivers ever"—became alive to the fact that something or somebody was knocking at her chamber window.

"In the name of wonder! what can this mean?" and the damsel began to quake. "My lucky stars forfend that this may be a witch or a warlock!"

It could not be Guy Gordon? And for a moment the face of Jean Graham was lighted up with love. Ah, no! The scanty bit of turf adhering to the strong wall under the window would not bear Guy's weight for the twentieth part of a second.

Plucking up some of the courage of which she was not generally wanting, Jean said—"I'll put the fiend to flight in Almighty's name ; no uncanny creature can withstand the mention of the Deity."

Slowly opening the little lattice, the startled maiden said—"In the name of God, depart in peace," and was closing the window more quickly than she had opened it, when she heard an anxious voice.

"It is I, it is I, Miss Graham—Gabrielle—Gabrielle Stuart."

"How got you, Gabrielle," said the much-alarmed young woman, "into this awful position ? You see I cannot get you between the too close stanchions, and you are sure, by one incautious step, to be dashed into a thousand pieces. O God, how came you here ?"

In little less time than we take to describe it, Gabrielle had delivered her message—"The Castle is beset : raise the

alarm at once!" and was soon safely back
once more on solid land.

Had it been daylight, it is unlikely that
the little lady could ever have made such a
dangerous venture. The yawning depth
below was enough to shake the strongest
nerve, to cause the coolest head to become
giddy. But now she was safe, and her first
act was to fall on her knees and thank the
Almighty for her almost miraculous escape
from a violent death.

Returning with less care than she had
displayed formerly, Gabrielle was alarmed
by the sudden challenge, "Who goes there?"

"Surely it cannot be wrong," she thought,
"to pretend to be what my loving mother
pretended;" and she answered firmly,
"Merely a strolling minstrel."

And Gabrielle gently touched the strings
of her lute.

"Silence!" said the soldier in a harsh
whisper, "or I may send an arrow through
thy little head. Thou art indeed a very
young strolling minstrel," added the soldier,

as he clutched her rudely. "At the dead of night strolling minstrels are usually kittle cattle. You must come to the captain of the guard."

And little Gabrielle was dragged before an officer, armed to the teeth, ready for the projected attack. On the ground lay men-at-arms either asleep or pretending to be so, but all around was quiet almost as the grave. After a few questions, the officer said—

"Let the little woman go; but see that she travels not towards the Castle. I trust that this ill-timed visit of the little gipsy may forebode no evil."

And Gabrielle sped like a young doe in the direction of Greyscaur.

.   .   .   .   .

Naturally enough, Jean Graham at once gave the alarm inside.

Quickly but quietly the slumbering inmates of Greenan Castle and its extensive policies were aroused. Within half an hour from the time that Gabrielle gave the alarm all were marching silently toward the Castle gate, each man having bow, sword, or arquebus, and some with all these implements of warfare attached by some means or other to their persons.

CHAPTER VII.

THE SORTIE.

" Oh, men ! what are ye. and our best designs,
  That we must work by crime to punish crime ?
  And slay, as if Death had but this one gate,
  When a few years would make the sword superfluous?"

Byron.

GABRIELLE got safely back to Greyscaur, where she was most affectionately received by all the members of the family. Apparently she was calm, but there was an excited gleam in the girl's eyes that told of the strain her nervous system had sustained during her short but perilous journey to the Castle.

Immediately after her return there was held a domestic council of war. It was first settled, and without dispute, that Guy Gordon should command the weak little garrison. that were in defence of the Home

Farm. Each man received a supply of ammu-
nition, and loaded his arquebus. Then Mrs
Marling and Gabrielle were placed in the
position of greatest safety, and all lights were
ordered to be extinguished, to give the house
a deserted appearance. Lastly, the utmost
silence was enjoined.

Meanwhile, the portcullis of the Castle had
been softly raised, and the armed men
marched as silently as possible across the
lowered drawbridge. Lord Kennedy personally superintended the entire arrangements.
When all his forces had been brought out,
with the exception of the few men necessarily
left to form a little garrison, Lord Kennedy
raised aloft his sword, and in stentorian tones
shouted—

"Every man for himself, and God for us
all! Down with the Crawfords!"

Then began the dreadful work of slaughter.
The would-be besiegers were taken completely
by surprise, and in the first few minutes,
being almost stupified, many of them were
actually slain before they could stand to their

arms. This opening advantage was sustained, as it usually is in such cases, throughout the entire strife.

The surprised enemy endeavoured to retire in order; but the success of the Kennedys made them still more anxious for further success, and a panic spread throughout the ranks of the terror-stricken foe.

"Down with the crafty Crawfords!" was the battle-cry. And down they went like grain before the scythe.

In great disorder, a section of them fell back on Greyscaur, where they thought they might fight under cover; but a murderous volley from the upper parts of the house so utterly discomfited the Crawfords and their allies that they retreated helter-skelter towards the sea-shore.

"The Kennedys take no quarter, and they give none!" was everywhere the cry, and for nearly two hours the horrible carnage went on unabated. Soon after morning broke, the smiling spring sun shone on a scene of the most awful description. The dying and the

dead lay huddled together in direful confusion; many of the slain still held each other
in the final death-grip; while weary, blood-
stained men-at-arms straggled by the shore,
or along the Roman road towards the town
of Ayr.

Alas poor Gabrielle! the sights she saw on
that same morning entirely shook her faith in
the humanity of man.

.   .   .   .   .

Many a day passed ere Greenan and its
immediate neighbourhood got rid of the
numerous death marks left by that dreadful
sortie. Since its occurrence Lady Kennedy
had been a confirmed invalid, and Gabrielle
had been her constant attendant. Every
effort had been made to keep hidden the fact
that Gabrielle had been the direct means of
saving the Castle and its defenders, but Jean
Graham was too much of a gossip to keep her
tongue still in such a remarkable matter.
The consequence was that, like all other so-
called secrets, Gabrielle's heroic deed got far
more publicity than if it had been given out

as a regular piece of public information. It was more than a nine days' wonder in the town of Ayr, while even in Glasgow the name of Gabrielle Stuart was for a time in every mouth.

Guy Gordon, too, came in for a considerable share of the approval of the numerous allies of the Kennedys. On the night of the sortie, after he found that Greyscaur was safe from further attack, Guy mounted his strong hunter, and followed in the hot pursuit of the enemy, among whom he made sad havoc. Twice, too, he courageously saved the life of Lord Kennedy himself.

A piece of grim humour, too, had cropped up in connection with the fearful slaughter. Tam M'Vulcan, the parish smith, with a huge broadsword, had gone about hacking and hewing in all directions. One poor fellow shouted to Tam, "Quarter, quarter!" But the blood-thirsty blacksmith, pretending not to understand, said, "I ha'e nae time to quarter ye, so I'll just cut ye in twa." And with one blow he severed the poor wretch's head from his body!

Lord Kennedy appeared to be the only person who appreciated not the noble act of our heroine and the daring deeds of Guy Gordon. He treated Gabrielle perhaps more coldly than ever; while she in turn showed towards him a *hauteur* which seemed strangely at variance with her youth and inexperience.

The fact of his Lordship's strong dislike to Gabrielle was soon pretty well known in the Castle, and naturally enough the knowledge thereof soon spread to Greyscaur. Mrs Marling, kind body, was an over-zealous Protestant, and she determined to turn Lord Kennedy's dislike to some account in the way of endeavouring to wean Gabrielle from her Papistical and, of course, in Mrs Marling's strictly Presbyterian eyes, utterly erroneous ways.

Hitherto Gabrielle had attended the Sunday ministrations of the Castle chaplain, who was known to have, like Lord and Lady Kennedy themselves, pretty strong Roman

Catholic leanings. But Mrs Marling made up her mind that the child should be plucked like a brand from the burning. And she was never done with worrying Mr Marling about the evils of Popery—a subject which he, good man, very properly cared nothing about.

"Just to fancy," Mrs Marling would say, "that anyone should be brought to the belief that a bit of common bread is the actual body of our Saviour, and that a drop of cheap wine is His real blood. The thing is perfectly shocking."

"But, my dear," Mr Marling would reply, "if that particular belief does its believers any particular good, I don't see why they shouldn't believe in it."

"What a piece of sophistry!" Sophistry was always a good word with Mrs Marling, although she had but a vague idea of its real meaning.

"But why, my dear wife, should there not be more than one road to heaven? Why should we eternally jostle each other by all taking the same route?"

Then Mrs Marling would hold up her
hands in holy horror, and call Mr Marling
a "heathen Pagan unbeliever."

It has been often said that whisky is the
main cause of the obstinate theology that
exists in Scotland; but in those days whisky
had not been invented. And yet theological
strife was even more bitter then than it is
now. The prevailing belief was and is that
the performance of certain duties at certain
times constitutes true religion. In fact, a
Scotchman has been heard to say to his son,
"D----n you, sir, say your prayers!"
While the same boy, when the inquiry was
made, "Why don't you ask a blessing?"
answered with much unction, "Because I
dinna like the look o' the tatties!"

Thus Mrs Marling did not like the look of
Roman Catholic potatoes, and, as we have
already said, she determined that Gabrielle
should be plucked like a brand from the
burning.

The Marlings regularly attended old Alloway Kirk, an ecclesiastical edifice since made

famous as the scene of the wonderful sight
seen by the celebrated Tam o' Shanter; and
Mrs Marling got her husband prevailed on to
consult the minister—or vicar, as was then
the term even in Scotland—of that ancient
building.

The Rev. Dr Branton—he had his degree
from Glasgow University—was a good specimen of the rare type of a country clergyman.
Devoted exclusively to no particular school
of theological thought, his Christianity was
of the broadest kind, and contained more of
a cheerful hopefulness and less of the fear of
damnation than one usually finds in the
clerical mind. He sent nobody to hell for
holding different opinions from his own.
Although he had a decided preference for the
path he had himself chosen, he believed, as
he had taught Mr Marling to believe, that
there was more than one road to heaven.
Dr Branton not only tolerated, but even re-
spected, all forms of religion that were based
upon a common Christianity. Would to God
that we had now-a-days a Dr Branton dotted

here and there over Scotland! What a glorious country it would be without its theological bitterness!

> " True religion
> Is always mild, propitiative, and humble;
> Plays not the tyrant, plants no faith in blood,
> Nor bears destruction on her chariot wheels,
> But stoops to polish, succour, and redress,
> And builds her grandeur on the public good."

But in many parts of Scotland true religion appears to be " Aff and up the Cowgate!"

Dr Branton, it was ultimately arranged, was to be invited to Greyscaur to dinner, when Gabrielle Stuart's present and future states were to be put before him, and his candid opinion asked on the same.

As Mrs Marling put it, "Gabrielle saved our bodily lives on that dreadful night of the sortie, and it is our duty, in return, to endeavour to save her eternal life."

But Mrs Marling, as will be seen in a future chapter, was reckoning without her host.

CHAPTER VIII.

"TO GLASGOW!"

"Honest good-humour is the oil and wine of a merry meeting, and there is no jovial companionship equal to that where the jokes are rather small and the laughter abundant."—*Washington Irving*.

" Through the shadow of the globe we sweep into the
    younger day ;
Better fifty years of *Glasgow* than a cycle of Cathay."
                                            Tennyson.

SCOTLAND, according to English — or rather, perhaps, Cockney—writers, has ever been guilty of displaying a decided want of humour. The Rev. Sidney Smith's "surgical-operation" joke is always being thrown in the teeth of the Scotch. Dr Samuel Johnson's bitter but innocuous Scotch sarcasms, too, are in England, especially in London, rejoiced over with great joy. But no men knew better than did Samuel Johnson and Sidney Smith that Scotland is essentially the land of dry wit and rich humour.

In the West of Scotland, especially, the inhabitants are not only humorous, but they are decidedly witty. Glasgow, thank goodness! cannot lay claim to any great proportion of the feeble style of "chaff" that is so prevalent in London; nor can it be said that the denizens of St Mungo indulge in the wild wordiness that characterises the so-called humour of the citizens of Dublin. Were my humble opinion asked, I should say that there is more genuine humour to be found between the Tweed and the Doon than can be heard from Berwick to Plymouth, or from Belfast to Cork. But, as my opinion has not been asked, I pass on to the further details of my story.

Charles the Second had returned. The King had got his ain again. He had come safely "ower the water." Consequently, revelry was the order of the day. And in those days revelry was indeed revelry. The merry Magistrates of Ayr, for example, simply enjoined their townsmen to get drunk. Not in the exact words I have used, but very nearly so.

The recommendation ran :—" Ye Kinge, our Sovereign Lord, having been restored to his rightful throne, ye Magistrates of Air, in solemn conclave assembled, do hereby intimate that ane feast or jollification be held for aucht days, from next Friday to ye Friday following, baith days inclusive."

As may be easily imagined, almost the entire nation took advantage of the license given forth by the authorities of every town of any note. The community was ripe for it. The unbending severity of eleven years of tyrannical Republicanism had paved the way for a burst of dissipation and debauchery. Strange, is it not? the perversity of human nature! As a Scotchman once cannily put it, " We could keep the Ten Commandments very nicely if the word *not* were kept out of each of them."

All over Scotland elaborate arrangements had been made to worthily, or perhaps it

might be better described unworthily, cele-
brate the joyous occasion. And for nearly
a couple of centuries afterwards the anniversary of the Restoration was observed as
a high festival throughout the Church of
England. Thanks, however, to the better
sense of Scotland, the Restoration orgies
were much earlier abandoned in our country.
And yet Caledonia cannot now be con-
gratulated very much on the character of her
Church festivals, seeing that the Scottish
nation is still cursed in the keeping up of
those half-yearly days of dissipation misnamed Sacramental Fasts.

.   .   .   .   .

Early one morning in the autumn of 16—
gay groups of pleasure-seekers might have
been seen streaming through the Main Street
of Newton-on-Ayr. Glasgow, it had been
announced, was likely to be the scene of
unwonted revelry, and many hundreds of
the inhabitants of the Auld Town and
county were proceeding Glasgow-wards. All
classes of the community were represented.

Gentle and simple, male and female—many being in the fantastic "mumming" dresses common at the time—rode or walked together; some jesting, some singing, some drinking, none crying; all, in fact, bent on what is termed unrestricted enjoyment.

Fortunately, or unfortunately—I will not venture to say which—whisky, as I have formerly stated, had not been invented, but flasks of usquebagh were being freely handed about among the pleasure-seekers. This liquour was mainly composed of rough French brandy, flavoured with raisins, cinnamons, and other spices.

"To Glasgow!" was ever and anon the cry from some of the more demonstrative of the merry multitude.

"Let's have a stave from you, Jock Mucklewut," said one. And Jock, without any pressing, sung, as Iago did,—

> " King Stephen was a worthy peer,
> His breeches cost him but a croun,
> He held them saxpence all too dear,
> And call'd the tailor thief and loon.

He was a wight of high renown,
And thou art but of low degree;
'Tis pride that pulls the country down;
Then tak' thine auld cloak about thee."

"Aye, John," said one, "your ain cloak is unco' like mine; it's auld enough."

"Yes, but, verra unlike yours, it's paid for," said John.

"And who may King Stephen have been?" asked another.

"What you can never be! he was a gentleman."

"I can hear," shouted Tam M'Vulcan, the smith, "that ye hae no' yet mended your manners, Mr Mucklewut."

"Wiser like," retorted John, "that you, Tam, were at hame mendin' your bellows; for yesterday, when I passed your forge, the bellows were whistling waur than the auld mare your man was shoeing."

"Dinna get drunk, John Mucklewut, before we're weel oot o' the toon," shouted Tam Currier, a tall fellow in a leathern jerkin and long leggings to match.

"I'll no' get drunk wi' a' I'll get frae you," was John's pert retort.

"Nor wi' a' ye are likely to pay for," returned the other.

"Weel, weel," said John, without taking the slightest offence, "there's little else but usquebagh to live for noo-a-days. We appear to hae come to a sad pass in auld Scotland. It's work when ye are young, starve when ye are auld, and then the ill place when ye die. Sae I'll just e'en tak' a drap wi' you, my friend, Tam Currier."

"All right, John," and the good-natured leather worker handed over his fat flask. "Ye're a real representative o' oor ain countrie. The Englishman prays for good living; The Irishman prays for fire-arms; but the Scotchman prays, 'O Lord, tak' everything frae everybody, and gie't a' to me.'"

"Ne'er ye mind," retorted John, as he took a hearty pull at the liquor; "it'll be a lang time ere *your* prayers will hae ony effect." And the laugh for the nonce went against the currier.

Thus the time was merrily passed as
the pleasure-seekers straggled gaily onward.
Soon they arrived at the pretty little royal
burgh town of Irvine. Of course, a halt was
called at this ancient and hospitable place,
the men of which were then so famous for
their handloom manufacture of book-muslins,
checks, jaconets, and such like useful and
luxurious articles ; while its lasses were no
less famous for their skill in plying the
needle on muslin webs.

Alas, however, for its handloom weaving !
Steam and Glasgow have long since left
Irvine in the lurch ; and now the inhabitants
of the quiet little town can only pride themselves in their excellent Educational Academy
and their rather handsome kirks. In days of
old a young handloom weaver was a worthy
match even for "the pride o' a' the toon ; "
now the maidens sing—

> " Oh, mither, ouybody, ouybody, onybody ;
> Oh, mither, onybody but a creeshy weaver."

After partaking of some of the hospitalities

of Irvine—all taking the advice of Shenstone,
and "seeking for freedom at an inn"—a
move was made towards the grounds of
Eglinton Castle, where there was "open
house" to all comers, in the shape of numerous tents or marquees, containing substan-
tial provisions, and with extensive sleeping
accommodation. Here many of the revellers
remained until the termination of the *fetes*,
but the main body, after a couple of hours'
halt, proceeded slowly towards Glasgow, here
and there arranging for a night's quarters
in the hospitable little towns and villages
that dotted the way.

Of course the good town of Kilwinning
came in for a share of the patronage of the
roysterers. Like Irvine, it was then a quiet-
going, steady place, with a famous Abbey,
on the site of which is now built the parish
church. Old "Mother Kilwinning"—for art
not thou the *mater* of Scottish Freemasonry?
—methinks I could have loved thee better
then, with thy quiet habits and rustic sim-
plicity, than now, with thy reekie coal pits

and shrieking locomotives. But we must necessarily pay the penalty of civilisation! Still, the penalty is a heavy one—sometimes greater than we can well afford to bear.

By noon of next day most of the roysterers had arrived in the ancient city with the Cathedral dedicated to St Mungo.

.   .   .   .   .

Glasgow at that time—as we have stated in a former chapter—gave but few evidences of its future great commercial prosperity. It is true that in outline, and from its position, there were plainly evident what the Scotch familiarly and truthfully term the "makings of a great city;" but the river was then, and for many years afterwards, in a sadly neglected state. Even as late as 1759, in an Act passed for improving the navigation of the Clyde, the preamble of the bill set forth that from Dumbuck to the bridge of Glasgow the water was so shallow in some parts that boats, barges, and other vessels could not pass to and from the city of Glasgow excepting during flood or spring tides. In fact, Port-

Glasgow was the place where vessels of any size loaded and unloaded.

Where are now the savage beauties of the Clyde? Where now the mysterious-looking bays and weird-like coves into which ancient Young Glasgow tremblingly pulled itself in tiny skiffs? Why, from the Broomielaw to Dumbarton Rock—last time I passed that way, and that is but a very short time ago—I could not espy a corner of the Clyde in which a well-doing mermaid might in peace and quietness, and as grey morning [dawns, lay down her weary head after a hard night's swim in search of errant sailors. Another shocking result of that civilisation which, in the matter of Clyde steamships, is paddling and screwing us, at the rate of upwards of twenty miles an hour, to the end of time!

Nought now on the queenly river but crowded paddle-steamers darting out of every creek, and leaving behind them long banners of black smoke; or huge screw liners, having on board hundreds of men and women going

off on voyages to some part or other of the
great Western Republic with as little ceremony, perhaps even less, than their forefathers
were wont to display on making a voyage to
the town of Greenock.

CHAPTER IX.

RESTORATION REVELRIES IN SANCT MUNGO.

"The greatness that would make us grave
Is but an empty thing:
What more than mirth would mortals have?
The cheerful man's a king!"

Bickerstaff.

GLASGOW was indeed gay. Every man as well as every woman was cheerful, and consequently every man as well as every woman was a king or a queen—at anyrate according to the great Bickerstaff.

The City of Sanct Mungo, which was then, as I have before stated, but ninth or tenth in importance of the towns of Scotland, could indeed be gay when it chose. It is true the West of Scotland has in modern days held one Tournament; but it was a very expensive affair, and marred by bad weather. Still, it showed great spirit on the part of the "good Earl," the late Lord Eglinton.

The Green, or Great Park as it was sometimes designated, was, at the Tournament in
16—, a perfect mass of bunting. Pavilions
and tents of all shapes and sizes were dotted
here and there over the huge expanse of turf.
Lists had been arranged, and the Grand
Tournament was about to be held.

For days many famed Scottish knights
had, as was the custom in those times,
publicly exhibited their shields for the
purpose of proving that they were good
men and true, and consequently fitted by
their rank to raise lances against men of
gentle blood.

From all quarters of Scotland, and from a
great many parts of England, thousands of
sightseers had come: and Glasgow was
crowded as Glasgow had never been crowded
before.   Dame and knight were there in
many hundreds, while the middle and lower
orders were present in many thousands.   On
the first morning of the Tournament all hied
them to the Green.   All were merry, and all
were orderly, for in those days the people

were necessarily much more temperate than they occasionally are at the present time.

To give some idea of the mixed wealth of the period, and the incongruity of the decorations then used, let us enter one of the numerous tents used for sleeping and other accommodation during the prescribed time of the revels.

What a strange mixture of luxuriousness and discomfort! Our knight is evidently a bit of an artist. The first thing that strikes the visitor is a gorgeous hearthrug, formed of a heavy leopard skin, which had been of great beauty until it was spoilt by wine stains and hot cinders. Some menial had evidently used the skin, in front of a fireplace, for his conjoined refreshment and sleeping accommodation. Fire-irons—at least those of an ordinary pattern—were wanting, but an Oriental scimitar, with a quaintly-carved handle, and a richly Damascened blade, much notched and battered in its new occupation, did duty for the absent fireplace utensils; while alongside was the cover of an old Greek vase, with a mythological "subject" in low relief running round the broad outer band.

Sitting accommodation was ample as to quantity, but very limited both as to capability of affording support, and as to freedom from other service. There was a fine old armchair, covered with green velvet, and having lions' heads boldly carved in black oak gazing with sleepy fixedness from beneath the stuffed arm cushions ; but that was not available as a seat, for it was filled to the top of its broad back with portfolios of engravings, old sketch books, and canvases of old "studies" tumbled together in a confused heap.

There were two other arm-chairs of ebony, relieved with bands and ornaments in tarnished gilding, and further adorned with curiously inlaid medallions of pottery; but of the two one wanted a seat and the other lacked a leg. There was also a priedieu, glowing in the richness of claret-coloured velvet and bullion fringe, but that was far more ornamental than useful. Then there

were two or three seats resembling modern
camp-stools, picturesquely upset in various
quarters of the tent, but of these, only one
was sound enough to bear any reasonable
weight.

The sides were variously ornamented. On
one some one had tried his hand at mural
decoration, and had failed ; and the failure
was only half hidden by some immense
knights and ladies, bishops and abbots,
robbed from some old ecclesiastical brasses
and pinned up, and by a collection of anti-
quated pikes and broad-swords, which had
been arranged star-wise as a trophy of arms,
though the effect had been spoilt by the
introduction of a stage-sword or two in
brilliant fancy scabbards, which had been
added in a barbaric moment, evidently " to
put a bit of life into the thing, and give it
warmth and colour."

Such is a somewhat crude description of
the interior of a Tournament tent or pavilion
at the Restoration Revels in the ancient city
of Glasgow. It was subject of remark that

the clergy did not take part in the rejoicings, as they had so long been in the habit of doing. But the Church had some time before placed its ban on the Tourney, and had actually refused to perform holy rites over the remains of any one whose life had been lost in the lists.

The people, however, were then throwing off the clerical swaddling-clothes in which they had been so long and so firmly wrapped; and no better proof could be given of the fact than the enormous concourse that had gathered at Glasgow to do fitting honour to the Restoration.

.   .   .   .   .

A blast of trumpets announced the arrival of the grand procession. It was headed by the "King" and the "Queen" of the Tournament, who were ushered into their thrones, in a large Gothic gallery or grand stand set aside for the nobility and gentry. Another blast of trumpets gave notice to contending knights that they should retire to their respective tents and arm for the fray.

When the knights came forth duly pre-
pared to give battle, the sight was exciting
and beautiful in the extreme. The armour
of the gentlemen and the caparisons of the
horses were of great grandeur and of the
most costly character. The mailed warriors
eyed each other defiantly through their
raised visors, while even their chargers
seemed to feel the important positions they
held in the Tourney, as they pawed the turf,
impatiently champed the bit, or repeatedly
tossed high their heads in nervous, spasmodic
jerks.

Some minor contests had taken place
without anything more serious having happened than that one knight was carried to
his tent in a semi-insensible condition, when
an excited "Hush!" seemed to universally
emanate from the vast assemblage. "Hush!"
and the proverbial pin would certainly have
been heard to make its proverbial fall.

A combatant who had refused to give his
name, but who had given the necessary
guarantee—through three knights of un-

questioned descent—that he was properly fitted to appear in the lists with combatants entitled to wear golden spurs, had challenged to mortal combat the Lord Kennedy of Castle Greenan. Lord Kennedy had accepted that challenge.

This arrangement was not in conformity with the strict rules of the present Tourney, as it was considered to be more an exhibition of skill and a trial of strength than a gathering to settle differences that required the death of one or both of those engaged in the contest. But the authorities had suddenly permitted the encounter, and the spectators, with that strange and morbid curiosity that is too frequently exhibited by the masses when life and death are immediately concerned, awaited the "mortal combat" with whetted interest.

The unknown knight, who rode into the lists with his visor closed, was magnificently mounted and accoutred. His suit of armour was made of pure Milan steel, burnished almost blue, and decorated with gold studs or rivets, curiously inlaid with the same costly metal, and exquisitely wrought in arabesque; while the bars of his carefully closed visor were of solid gold.

Lord Kennedy was more modestly, but quite as substantially, armed and horsed for the combat. He rode into the lists with visor raised, and with a defiant smile on his very determined, but very pale, countenance.

The two knights rode into the middle of the lists, bowed deeply to the King and the Queen of the Tournament, and then haughtily to each other. Each then retired to the extreme of his own position. Then a herald shouted, "*Laisser les allez!*" (Let them go), and the trumpets sounded the charge.

The result was almost electrical. Like a couple of arrows from strongly-strung bows, the horses, spurred into fury, almost flew towards each other. Then a dreadful shock, a fierce shout, a loud huzza, and both riders are unhorsed at the same moment. God help us! Are they both killed? No, no. When each of the combatants rises angrily from the ground he seems almost as hale and hearty as if he had never been struck. They are both tall, well-built, strong men ; the Unknown is, however, much the younger and the handsomer of the two.

They have their battle-axes handed to them, and then begins the more serious part of the conflict. A few passes and the Lord Kennedy, seeing an advantage, makes a left-handed lounge at the breast-plate of his opponent. The Unknown simply skips aside from the blow that would more than likely have bereft him of life, and with an arm like Samson, and as quick as lightning—while he shouts, "*En Dieu est ma fiance*"—he cleaves the helmet of Lord Kennedy as it were a piece of delf, and his Lordship falls to the ground like a heap of lifeless clay.

Lord Kennedy's attendants carry him at once from the field—bleeding, insensible, and evidently in the very jaws of death. The great crowd shouts applause, the heralds order the retiring blast of trumpets, and

everybody, of course feels happy that somebody has been killed—killed dead, and no
mistake !

And Lord Kennedy's gasping and bleeding
body is ultimately carried away to the house
of an apothecary in the Gorbals, then merely
a few houses called Bridgend, and belonging
to the parish of Govan.

Next day the Tournament authorities,
backed by the Church authorities, and
"endorsed" by the Magisterial authorities,
arrange that there shall be no further
Tourney. They command that the revels
shall be carried out in other and more
agreeable ways. There may be death—
slow death—in the cup, but that, the great
authorities think, is better than sudden
death by the axe. There may be baiting
of beasts and killing of birds; but such are
merely "sports." Then go on with the riot
and the revels.

  .   .   .   .   .

That night of the Tourney strange sights
and sounds were seen and heard in the

little district called the Gorbals and its neighbourhood.

The apothecary, into whose grim house the maimed body of Lord Kennedy was carried, was generally considered an "uncanny" man. It was generally believed indeed that he had dealings with the imps of darkness.

At anyrate, loud shouts of sardonic laughter were heard to issue from the house; and just before daybreak a full-rigged brig, in a blaze of fire from her topmasts to her water-line, and steered by the Prince of Darkness himself, was seen by some good gossips to glide rapidly down the Clyde.

CHAPTER X.

"THE TWA CRONIES."

"Tam lo'ed him like a very brither;
They had been fou for weeks thegither."

Burns.

CIVILISATION has brought many good things in its train, but to Scotland it cannot be said to have brought any great measure of sobriety. Why? Nobody knows. The Church wags its head sapiently against the sad spectacle of intemperance, and goes on thumping the dry bones of doctrinal theology. The State goes on increasing the taxation on alcoholic drinks, while the people go on drinking all the more, and the Exchequer sadly—so, at least, the Chancellor himself says—but certainly pockets the ill-gotten proceeds. Magistrates make restrictive by-laws and close the back-doors of public-houses, but the people walk in boldly by the front.

Something can, indeed, be said for the "good old times," even the good old times as they existed in the West of Scotland. In the village of Greenan there was, at the time of our tale, but one ale-house. And a comfortable little place it was. It was kept by Mrs M'Mutchkin, the widow of a fisherman who had lost his life off the fishing village of Dunure during the prevalence of a violent storm.

Some three or four years after the events detailed in our last chapter, Tam M'Vulcan, the village blacksmith, and Jock Mucklewut, the village glazier, and general man-of-all-work, had forgathered—as we say in Scotland —at Lucky M'Mutchkin's house of call, where they sat in the cozy apartment that served at once as kitchen, dining-room, and parlour. On the dresser-shelves were rows of shiny plates, and above the fire-place (in which merrily burned a huge log of wood) were dozens of burnished dish-covers.

It was not by any means the first time the two worthies had met in the same place. In fact, their first meeting at the guidwife's house had been a memorable one. They were the actors in what has since become a good Scotch story.

The blacksmith had but newly come to the village, and the glazier, finding Tam a congenial fellow, was determined to "take him by the hand." Accordingly, one night, after sitting long "boozin' at the nappy," and having heard Tam complain sadly of want of work, Jock went mysteriously out of the ale-house. Returning in about half an hour, he said, whisperingly—

"Tam, I've done you a guid turn; ye'll soon get plenty o' work. I've broken every ploughshare I could find in the neighbourhood."

Tam, with tears of gratitude and "tippenny" in his eyes, immediately ordered in another stoup o' reamin' swats. Moreover, and not to be outdone in generosity by the good glazier, Tam in a short time also went out mysteriously. On his return the blacksmith exclaimed—

" I've gi'en ye as much work as ye've gi'en me. I've broken every pane o' glass in the Parish Kirk."

"Lord, man," shouted the dumfoundered glazier, "I keep the glass o' the kirk in repair by contract!"

.   .   .   .   .

On the night of the present forgathering, the subject of this chapter, the conversation turned upon our heroine and the Kennedy family. Gabrielle, now a young woman of transcendent loveliness, but still with a tinge of melancholy on her beauteous features, lived almost altogether at the Castle nursing Lady Kennedy.

" I often meet the Flower o' Castle-Greenan," said Mucklewut, " walking wi' Lord Charles Montgomery, the nephew and heir o' the Earl o' Eglinton."

" And so do I, Jock. D'ye think they'll mak' a match o't ? "

" Whist, whist, ye haveril ! She's a Roman

and he's now become a Protestant. Besides, it's said that, when Lady Kennedy dies, Miss Gabrielle means to enter a convent in France and devote a' her days to religion."

"Ah, weel, weel; rather her than me. But it looks as if she devoted a lot o' time already to that same business. She's ower often, I fancy, wi' that auld Roman sneck-drawer, Father Garthwaite."

"Tuts, tuts, man; when the young lady gangs to Garthwaite's cottage it's mainly to attend on his old housekeeper, Nancy, wha's nearly auchty year auld; and a bitter auld Roman she is."

"Weel, weel, never mind," said the jolly smith; "Miss Gabrielle, Roman or no' Roman, is the bonniest lassie I ever saw; so let us e'en drain a stoup to her."

"Wi' a' my heart," responded the quite as jolly man-of-all-work; "and as Lord Charles is a braw lad, and a guid lad, let us couple their names thegither. As the old ballad has it—

'His step is first in peacefu' ha',
His sword in battle keen.'"

And the two roysterers emptied a special stoup to the toast.

"And what d'ye think, Jock, Lord Kennedy 'll say to a' this when he comes ower frae the Lady Isle?"

"He'll ne'er be ower frae the Lady Isle. He's as mad as a March hare."

"Aye, man; I'm tauld that the ongauns o' his Lordship and that auld Glasgow apothecary are somthing awfu'. They drink and blaspheme in the most terrible manner. And they say that Lord Kennedy had half o' his head and mair than half o' his brains carried off on that day o' the Tourney."

"Nonsense, Tam, nonsense; how could a man exist wi' only half o' his head. and less than half o' his brains?"

"Oh, ye ken, they say the auld apothecary invoked the aid o' Auld Nick himsel', and between them they kept my lord alive, and in the end made a sort o' cure o' him. I ken that on that night o' the Tourney, when John Vass, the fisherman, was drawin' his fishin' lines just off the Heads o' Ayr, a coach-and-four came driving through the water, quite close to the boat in which John an' his four companions were at their night's work. An' there, on the box-seat, sat Auld Clootie breathin' black smoke from his fiery nostrils. John Vass, in awfu' fear, shouted, 'From whence to where?' An' Clootie, in a voice like thunder, answered, 'From hell to Lord Kennedy's burial!'"

"Dinna blether, man, Tam; dinna blether. D'ye think the devil's such a fool as to yoke his horses for nothing? He would ken fine whether Lord Kennedy was dead or no'."

"But it was perhaps the invocation o' the infernal apothecary that made Auld Hughie change his mind. This I do ken, that the coach-and-four, wi' the horses sending sheets o' fire frae their wide-spread nostrils, drove rapidly round the Heads; and the noise the fiery chariot made as it rushed through the water was just, by a' the world, like the roarin' o' the Bars o' Ayr. Then it took a' the usquebagh in John's boat to keep the men frae fainting clean awa'."

"Aye, aye," said Mucklewut, dryly, "there's far ower much usquebagh about the story."

But the doughty blacksmith, not to be put down, returned to the charge.

"Perhaps, Jock, ye'll no' believe the story about Lord Kennedy's big Bible; but I ken it's true, for ane that was present tell't me a' about it."

"Go on with it; if it be like the other story, I'll no' believe a single word of it."

"Weel," proceeded the blacksmith, "at ane o' their awfu' midnight orgies on Lady Isle, the apothecary and his Lordship arranged that Skipper Park and four men should man a boat, and that Lord Kennedy's swearin' man-servant should take the big Bible under his arm, gang on board the boat, and drop the Bible into the sea at the distance of about a mile frae the island."

"Lord, man, Tam, ye mak' a body's flesh creep. Here, Luckie M'Mutchkin, bring anither stoup o' swats, and put a wee drap usquebagh into it. The drink wants strength."

Tam went on, "Weel, ye see, when they had rowed out about a mile, and when the man-servant was just gaun to drop the Bible into the sea, he was struck dead by a flash o' lightning—aye, as dead's a herrin'."

"And nobody else in the boat hurt?" anxiously asked the incredulous glazier.

"Not one. I have Skipper Park's solemn word for the entire story. Moreover, the big Bible was never seen again, and the man-servant's dead body never stiffened."*

"For Godsake, Tammas, stop it! Rather let us have a song, and be done with that gruesome story."

And Tam, noway loth, and in stentorian

---

* There is not a great deal of imagination in this story. The present writer, forming one of seven, including two Ayr fisherman—both highly respectable and sober men—was once in a boat near Lady Isle, when the electric fluid splintered the boat's mast, and killed one of the fishermen as he sat quietly smoking his pipe. Neither the boat itself, nor any other of its occupants, were injured. As to the man-servant's body never stiffening, that is alleged to be the case with every animal so bereft of life.

strains, gave the following bacchanalian song,
which I will take the liberty of entitling

"FILL A BUMPER."

Fill a bumper, banish grief :
    Canting hypocrites despise;
Sorrow ne'er can give relief,
    Joys from drinking do arise ;
Why should we, with gloomy care,
Change what Nature made so fair ?
Chorus—Drink, and set your heart at rest :
    Of bad bargains make the best !

Some can think on nought but wealth,
    Some to honours do aspire ;
Give me brandy, give me health—
    That's the sum of my desire ;
What the world can more present
Will not add to my content !
Chorus—Drink, and set your heart at rest,
    And hypocrites can do their best !

Mirth, when mingled with good wine,
    Makes our hearts alert and free :
Let it rain, or snow, or shine,
    Draw a pint of wine for me !
There's no fence against our fate—
Changes daily on us wait.
Chorus—Drink, and set your heart at rest,
    Merry first, then do your best.

Other congenial spirits soon joined the twa cronies, and the night went on "wi' sangs and clatter" until the short hours of the morning, when Luckie M'Mutchkin insisted on the roysterers going to their respective places of abode.

CHAPTER XI.

LOVE.

" He knew whose gentle hand was at the latch
    Before the door had given her to his eyes;
And from her chamber-window he would catch
    Her beauty farther than the falcon spies;
And constant at her vespers would he watch,
    Because her face was turn'd to the same skies;
And with sick longing all the night outwear
To hear her morning step upon the stair."

Keats.

WHAT is the mysterious influence that is called love. Whence does it spring? How does it grow? Blatant orators, when vainly endeavouring to prove that the soul is as mortal as the body, never take love into account; yet it comes unbidden, and it cannot be ordered to depart. It is said that when poverty comes in at the door love flies out of the window. But I have a strong impression that such is not the case except in very exceptionable circumstances. Poverty, in my humble opinion, generally cements more strongly the passion existing between a loving pair. But perhaps it were better not to discuss the subject, and leave each respective individual to his or her own actual experience in the matter.

Gabrielle—our Gabrielle!—was in love. She could not help it. It came, she knew not why; and it obstinately refused to go. All her efforts to uproot it from her heart were unavailing. And no wonder.

Here was Lord Charles Montgomery, a handsome, well-behaved young man, very little older than herself, evidently thrown in her way by Lady Kennedy. In fact, her Ladyship's most particular care seemed to be to fan the flame that required no fanning whatever; for there it was, blazing merrily.

And he was as much in love as she. He was never thoroughly happy but in her presence. Her every wish it was his utmost pleasure to gratify; and his father gladly sanctioned his son's almost unlimited residence at Castle Greenan, simply stipulating that he should appear at Eglinton once a week. He had every confidence in the care and attention of Lady Kennedy, as he had known her from the days of her childhood. Indeed, they had almost been brought up together.

Thus, the course of the true love that existed between Charles and Gabrielle appeared to run smooth. But, alas, appearances —especially love appearances—are deceitful. When the water is at its smoothest, all at once it comes upon a chasm which sends it bounding angrily down hill, or it may be that it strikes a huge boulder and gets rudely tossed aside.

The young man's birth was enshrouded in mystery. His uncle, Lord Eglinton—or, to be correct, the Earl of Eglinton and Winton— was a misanthrope. In his time the Earl had taken part in the numerous broils of the period, and had been the deadly enemy of Lord Kennedy ; but for some years he had seldom gone beyond the boundaries of his own policies. He devoted himself mainly to study, and was generally understood to be deeply learned.

On one occasion he absented himself from the Castle for about a month. On his return he brought with him a boy, who, he said, was his nephew; and no one dared to dispute the statement, or make inquiries as to its truth or otherwise.

On the education of young Charles Montgomery the Earl had for several years spent most of his time; and the youngster, being of a studious disposition, ultimately became a worthy pupil of his learned uncle. In form Charles was particularly handsome; in personal stature he was perhaps a little more than the average; he had a profusion of jet-black curly hair; but, best of all—and this was the great charm in the eyes of Gabrielle —his heart was in the right place. He was courageous and kindly, while he was equally affable to poor and rich.

Moreover, the young nobleman was beneficent and benevolent. Let not the reader

misunderstand me.   Beneficence cannot always boast of a strictly honourable descent.
It may at times be the offspring of pride, of
self-conceit, of obligation, or of a conscience
that has been pricked into giving by the
remembrance of former iniquities.   Benevol-
ence, on the contrary, is of celestial birth;
for no by-ends can be attributed to the
Almighty.

Gabrielle, physically and mentally, was in
no respect inferior to her lordly lover.   Her
face and figure were exquisitely formed, while
a certain Gallic style about her seemed as if
her garments "tried to shade those beauties
which they could not hide."   Her rich flaxen
hair fell in profusion over her fair shoulders,
while her tiny feet keeked bewitchingly from
beneath her pretty purple kirtle.

By Father Garthwaite Gabrielle's young
mind had been amply stored with knowledge—religious, general, and useful.   Moreover, she had the knowledge that taught her
to know herself—a somewhat rare mental
commodity among our modern women.   It is

true that Gabrielle had been brought up in the Roman Catholic faith; but was not Lord Eglinton Catholic at heart, although for political reasons he made an ostensible show of Protestantism?

Finally, the courtship was fomented and fostered by Lady Kennedy, and formally approved of by the noble Earl himself.

Tale have I none to tell concerning the course of this happy and at one time likely-to-be-lasting affection. There were no rivals in the field; there was neither coquetry nor flirtation. It was a matter of mutual liking, and each endeavoured to make the other happy, in the hope that by beginning life well they would so end it.

Besides, they had before them the unhappy, the absolutely miserable married life of the Lady Kennedy, who for a long period had never seen, and very seldom even heard from, her now dreadfully dissipated husband.

It was plainly evident, too, to the youthful pair, that there existed some annoying secret, matrimonial or otherwise, that weighed heavily on the mind of the Earl himself. He gave way to fits of melancholy that not unfrequently lasted for days.

Gabrielle and her lover, happy in themselves, made each other still more happy in doing good to others. The poor and the needy ever found in them good friends; while they regularly frequented the bedsides of the afflicted.

Moreover, each taught the other; and both were in the highest degree intelligent for their years. Father Garthwaite's lessons were never lost. They indeed did more than perhaps they were intended to accomplish.

Charles Montgomery was fast returning to the Catholic faith of his fathers. And it is not to be wondered at when one considers the charming influence likely to be used by a descendant of the maligned Mary Stuart, for Gabrielle had all the actual virtues of her great ancestor, without a tinge of her alleged vices—all her sparkling humour, without a shadow of her bitter, biting sarcasm.

And then Charles Montgomery grew poetically sentimental. All young men become so when they are in love ; at anyrate, a large majority of them affect loving versification. Take a couple of verses from one of the "sentimentalities" of young Charles :—

THE BLUSH AND THE SMILE.

Oft, oft as I wander at gloamin' beside her,
   Far down in the dell where we plighted our love,
Her dimpled cheeks glow as I tell her, my treasure,
   How fondly I love and how constant I'll prove.
The nightingale sings its sweet sang to the e'enin',
   The stars in the blue lift look down a' the while,
And my heart throbs wi' joy as, wi' innocence beamin',
   My lassie looks up wi' a blush and a smile.

I care not for courts, and I long not for splendour,
   To me sordid wealth cannot happiness bring ;
Give gold to the great to assist in their grandeur—
   A rustic to me is far more than a king.
Then here I'll content me to woo my ain lassie,
   Whose charms are all sweetness, who never knew guile.
Then here's to her health in an o'er-brimming tassie—
   The maiden who loves wi' a blush and a smile.

I cannot pretend to say that the foregoing verses would have been worthy of Robert

Burns; but for a scion of nobility, and only out of his teens, they may pass muster even among the galaxy of poets and philosophers that have for many generations been produced by Paisley!

Poets and philosophers in Paisley! Why, as soon as a young man—even one who is not in love—arrives at Paisley railway station, even the sight of the frowning jail makes him begin to feel poetical and philosophic!

My readers will observe that Charles Montgomery has introduced the nightingale into his song. To save the time of adverse critics I may state that in those days there really were nightingales—Scottish nightingales, of course—in the West of Scotland.

CHAPTER XII.

ANCIENT SPORT IN "AULD KILLIE."

" We ought never to sport with pain and distress in any of our amusements, or treat even the meanest insect with wanton cruelty."—*Blair*.

" And now I will unclasp a secret book,
And to your quick-conceiving discontent
I'll read you matter deep and dangerous."
Shakespeare.

TO me it seems that civilisation has not permeated very deeply into our outdoor sports—as far, at least, as the inferior animal is concerned. It is true that now-a-days we do not bait bulls or bears—excepting on the Stock Exchange. But what about stag and fox hunting? and hare and rabbit coursing?

Some sapient persons have the audacity to say that stags and foxes rather like to be hunted. But I have not yet met a stag or a fox that said so. I have it, however, on no mean authority, that *post-mortem* examinations of coursed hares and rabbits have not unfrequently shown that the hearts of the wretched animals have burst through the terrible agony involved in the ordeal of coursing.

Dr Watts has told us that "dogs delight to bark and bite," and Dr Thomas Guthrie was wont to state that salmon liked to be hooked; but the dog who is being worsted in the battle ought to have *his* say; and if the salmon likes hooking, he takes a strange way of showing his liking by making strenuous, in fact almost superhuman, efforts to get clear away from his would-be captor.

.   .   .   .   .

In one of the horse-back outings so frequently indulged in by Charles Montgomery and Gabrielle Stuart they came one day, in the suburbs of Kilmarnock, on a great field of forty acres, where all ranks of society were represented, and in which the then great game of cock-fighting was being carried on in all the integrity which legalisation then unfortunately gave it.

(Thank goodness, that field—now called
the Kay Park—is at the present day devoted
to much nobler purposes. Game-cocks have
given way to healthy children ; blackguardism
has given way to education.)

As I have said, *all* classes were represented
at this then popular gathering. There was
the knight with his golden spurs, and the
weaver with his red-tasselled cowl.

"Mains" were being fought in various
parts of the field, the cocks having first been
weighed and matched to a nicety, and then
having "steel-heels" attached to their spurs,
the more effectually to kill their adversaries.

It is said in the case of game-cocks—and
their eagerness for the fray goes somewhat
to prove the statement—that they really
enjoy fighting, as horses often show that
they rack themselves in endeavouring to get
first to the winning post. But when a
disabled but still somewhat active game-
cock is put down on the ground that he
may be "practised on" by some strong
and healthy antagonist—as was the rule

—the sight is sickening, and cruel in the extreme.

Gabrielle had only been present on the field a few minutes, when she earnestly exclaimed,

" For the love of heaven, let us leave this terrible scene."

And yet the scene itself was picturesque enough in all conscience.

There, in one part of the field, accompanied by some of his wives and followers, was Johnny Fa', Lord and Earl of Little Egypt— otherwise King of the Gipsies—who bore a Privy Seal grant to do very much as he chose with the property of other persons, even to the extent of taking with impunity their lives !

The Gipsy King was fantastically dressed, and with huge gold rings in his ears. He was rather a handsome man, of a mixed Egyptian and Ethiopian cast of features. But his wives and women followers were a motley-looking lot, and not of the highest stamp of beauty, which may be one great reason for Johnny Fa' having extended his love favours to many ladies of high degree in England as well as Scotland.

As Charles and Gabrielle were slowly walking their horses from the crowded field, the King and his followers made a low obeisance; while suddenly one of the woman, with a skill worthy of a better cause, drew off Gabrielle's riding-glove, and looked closely into the palm of her hand.

Gabrielle, half-amused and half-offended, reined up her horse, and waited to hear her "fortune" told.

The ever-ready black-eyed Bohemian, with a subdued start, real or affected, half-spoke half chanted—

> "Methinks on this fair palm I plainly see
> Signs of the cruel curse of Kennedy."

Gabrielle, now really offended, indignantly withdrew her hand, and exclaimed,

"Begone, wretched woman! I'll have nought of thee or thy wicked divinations."

The Gipsy merely bowed her dusky head, and slowly exclaimed—

" But plainer still I see, as thy palm saith,
   Thy wedding will be brought about by death."

Charles Montgomery here tossed the woman a silver piece, and he and Gabrielle rode off at a quick pace.

But Gabrielle, strong-minded as she was, could not get the untoward circumstance eradicated from her recollection. For days subsequently there rang in her ears the solemn strains of the Gipsy woman—

"Thy wedding will be brought about by death."

CHAPTER XIII.

A MISSION OF MERCY.

"Who hath woe? who hath sorrow? who hath con-
tentions? who hath babbling? who hath wounds without
cause? who hath redness of eyes?   They that tarry long
at the wine; they that go to seek mixed wine.   .   .   .
It stingeth like an adder; it biteth like a serpent."—
Solomon.

> I hold it true, whate'er befall—
> I feel it when I sorrow most—
> 'Tis better to have loved and lost
> Than never to have loved at all.
> *Tennyson.*

SOME one—I fancy it was Bulwer Lytton
—has told us to beware of a man who
has been badly treated in his childhood. I
don't believe the suggestion is correct. Not
that I would advocate ill-treatment of children, but that children who have been ill-
treated do not, as a rule, ill-treat their own
or other children.   Doubtless, when the bairn

is born of vicious parents—which in my experience I have found a too common cause—he or she is sure in time to put in force that horrible law called the law of retaliation, even when there is little reason for so doing.

France, I fancy, is the country above all others in which I have been that is kindest to its infants. Scotland—I am almost ashamed to write the words—is far behind France in respect to its care of the little ones. Do not, gentle reader, think that I have the slightest idea that there is more affection in France than there is in Scotland. But there is much less drunkenness. God knows that, without whisky, Scotland's hardy and industrious sons would have made themselves the most successful, and their country perhaps the greatest, in the world.

At the present time, and on any Saturday night about eleven o'clock, take a look at the High Street of Edinburgh, one of the most lovely cities in the world. There you may witness scenes of drunkenness and consequent cruelty that will make your heart bleed. And this is the country of John Knox!

I am not endeavouring to try the high moral dodge. Without drunkenness there could be no sobriety; without poverty there could be no riches; without sin there could be no righteousness. But without whisky Scotland would have been a much better land, notwithstanding the well-known couplet—

> " Wi' tippeny we fear nae evil,
> Wi' usquebagh we'll face the devil."

There was a certain poor family at Greenan that had been utterly ruined by the indulgence of the parents in usquebagh and tippeny. A communication received by Lady Kennedy one day caused her to request Gabrielle and her lover to go to the village and find out the position of affairs in this alleged-to-be wretched house. Gladly the loving pair undertook the task, as they ever did when anything likely to involve a mission of mercy was concerned.

Would that our present system of education

was so arranged that our youth were more generally brought up to a more general love of their frailer fellow-creatures! It is only, I am sorely afraid, the few who fancy that kindness is far before sternness in bringing about good results, more especially among children. Now-a-days it is quite fashionable, even on the bench, where better example might be expected, to sentence children to be beaten. God knows, if we were all beaten for our every-day transgressions, there would soon be a decided scarcity of birch rods in the land!

They found the place a miserable little "but-and-ben," which at night covered the heads of a father and mother and eight children. The father was at Luckie M'Mutchkin's getting drunk as best he could; some of the elder children were at work in the fields, others were at play; a little ragged boy (with the face of an old man) sat looking sadly at the few dying embers of a cold fire; the mother lay on the floor of the kitchen dead drunk; and even she was not the worst sight in all that disgraced and degraded house.

It was the *aged* boy, somewhat under six years, seated by the side of that cold, cold hearth, who was the saddest spectacle in the sad place.

"Oh, God! what a sight!" exclaimed Gabrielle, as mixed tears of indignation and compassion filled her lovely eyes.

"What is your name?" she asked kindly of the boy.

"Willie," he answered, as he turned to Gabrielle, surprised that a real lady should address him kindly.

"Well, Willie, come away with me; I will take you out of this dreadful den and have you cared for."

"I cannot leave *her*," he said, without even looking towards his debauched mother; "I cannot leave *her*. She is very, very good when she is not drunk."

There was a painful pause. The child was plainly weeping, but no tears came from his wearifully-sad eyes. The cruelty to which

the poor boy had been subjected had posi-
tively dried up the fountain of relief that
so often plays consolatory tears among the
young.

"Charles, Charles," said Gabrielle, "say,
in God's name, what is to be done in connection with this fearful case?"

"Let us first forcibly remove the child,
and pay some neighbour to wait upon this
unfortunate woman."

"But I cannot leave *her*," again came from
the lips of the little one; "I cannot leave *her;*
she is very good when she is not drunk."

"But when is she not drunk?" anxiously
inquired Charles.

"When the money is all done, and the
clothes all sold. She will likely be good
to-morrow. Oh, mother, mother, what a
terrible life!" he wailed piteously.

And the child shook and shuddered as if
he would die.

The peculiar wailing sound of the boy's
voice had evidently brought back a portion
of the sodden senses of the besotted mother.

Raising herself on one elbow, she stared wildly, first at the strange visitors, and then angrily at the little age-stricken boy.

Through her dishevelled and matted hair could be discerned features that had once been actually of a superior order; but strong drink had done its dreadful work so thoroughly that there was nought but the merest wreck of what had once been one of the Almighty's fairest creatures.

With drunken knowingness the woman got to her feet, and staggering towards her child, she exclaimed harshly, "What are you whining at, you daft brat?" and with one fierce blow she felled the boy into the fire-place.

Then, quickly realising what she had so suddenly done, with a loud shriek the wretched drunkard fell fainting on the inaminate body of her too-loving child.

   ·   ·   ·   ·   ·

For days and days the poor child's life hung trembling in the balance—the border land between life and death. Ultimately he recovered; but, alas! it could then be plainly seen that the aged boy would never become an aged man or even a sane man.

.   .   .   .   .

Yet I will be told that the foregoing is a fancy picture—a piece of exaggeration dragged in for sensational purposes. But it is unfortunate that I myself saw such a scene as that I have endeavoured to describe. I say "endeavoured to describe," for no human hand could thoroughly depict on paper the fearful horrors of that terrible house and the dreadful daily sufferings of those eight innocent children.

Year after year the awful work of moral and physical destruction had been going on in that miserable house, and it was only by public attention having been drawn to the matter, and the parents incarcerated that they might be saved from themselves and their children, that a gleam of social sunshine beamed upon those wretched weans.

But many thousands of such cases—cases, too, in which the sunshine never shows itself—

are going on in this country every day ; ay, every day.

.   .   .   .   .

"Will *she* be back soon?" asked little Willie, as Gabrielle brought him flowers into the pretty little room in which he was ensconced at Greyscaur. "Oh, Miss Gabrielle, I love her so very much. And then she is so very good when she is not drunk.

"She will be back soon, dear Willie ; wait patiently until you are once more well, and you will see your mother again. Let us pray, Willie, that she will always be good in future. God is the hearer and answerer of prayer."

And Gabrielle, on her knees, prayed fervently that the Almighty would reclaim that wretched woman and make her a comfort to her afflicted boy. Then Gabrielle fondled the aged child until he sunk into a semi-slumber.

"I'll see her soon again, I'll see her soon again," murmured the half-sleeping child. "Oh, mother, mother, why do you drink that dreadful poison? Why is it permitted to be made? And you are so very good when you are not drunk."

Poor Willie, poor Willie; you are not old enough to know that your wretched mother is no exception to the rule. We are all, or most of us, very good when we are not drunk.

CHAPTER XIV.

MYSTERY.

" A kind of weight hangs heavy at my heart ;
My flagging soul flies under her own pitch,
Like fowl in air too damp, and lugs along
As if she were a body in a body,
And not a mounting substance made.
My senses, too, are dull and stupified,
Their edge rebated, Sure some ill approaches—
A spirit tells me that some Fate's at hand."

Dryden.

LITTLE WILLIE'S progress towards re-
covery was very slow.   Three times every
day he was visited by Gabrielle ; in fact, all
the time that she could spare from Lady Kennedy's room and from her lover was devoted
to attendance on the boy.   And he was not
ungrateful to Gabrielle for her more than
ordinary kindness.   He always became rest-
less when she was expected to pay him a
visit, and his eyes glistened with inward
satisfaction when she entered his chamber.

One evening in December, after having taken her departure for Greyscaur on her usual visit to Little Willie, the domestics at Castle Greenan became alarmed at Gabrielle's unusually prolonged absence.

After a time Lady Kennedy was informed of the circumstance, and she too becoming alarmed, at once commanded that a messenger should be despatched through the woods to the Home Farm. Soon he returned with the surprising intelligence that Gabrielle had not been at Greyscaur since mid-day, and that the aged boy was getting rapidly worse.

Then numerous messengers were sent to scour the country. But all to no purpose. At last there was no blinking the fact. Gabrielle had disappeared in a most un-accountable manner, and not the slightest clue was left to indicate her whereabouts.

.   .   .   .   .

That night a stranger—a foreigner evidently —called at Greyscaur, and desired to be directed to the cottage of Father Garthwaite. Young Tom Marling was sent with the

stranger, who seemed a gentleman by
education and manners. But young Tom
got afraid of the foreigner. Several distinct
suspicions concerning the stranger passed
rapidly through his mind. In the first place,
it was an unusual circumstance to find an
utter stranger in Greenan at all, and it was
especially strange for one to penetrate
unnoticed so far into the recesses of Greyscaur
woods, which contained no public paths, and
which were removed a mile or two from the
public highway.

Then the man was plainly not an Englishman ; who could tell what burglarious or
even murderous intentions his mind might
harbour ? His costume was, indeed, that of
a gentleman ; but was it likely that a gentleman would go roaming about by himself on
private property, without permission, and
selecting the least frequented paths ?

Tom hardly knew how to set his suspicions
at rest, and his sense of propriety, small as it
was, prevented him from trying to cross-
examine the stranger, but at the same time

he thought he could do no harm by throwing
out a few general hints by way of warning.
So, in the most casual and unpremeditated
manner that he could assume, Tom commenced—

"You see that post there? P'raps you
don't know what it's for? It's a gibbet
where they hang people for burglary, or
felony, or larceny, or anything wicked."

The stranger did not even make an exclamation of surprise. So Tom returned to
the charge in another way.

"There used to be, too, a good deal of
poaching about here years ago, but that's
nearly all gone off. You see there are such
heaps of game that people thought nothing
of knocking it over, but now it's all strictly
preserved, and the magistrates are severe
on poachers."

But the stranger still kept up his quiet,
almost gloomy, style, and spoke not a word.

At length they reached the priest's cottage,
and Tom's suspicions were soon removed when
he saw the cordial warmth with which the

priest and the stranger met, for it was evident that they were old friends.

And, indeed, Tom felt rather ashamed of himself when, in answer to the query, " How did you find your way here ? " the stranger replied, with a good-natured pat on the lad's head, " I lost myself in a neighbouring wood, but this young gentleman came to my help ; and though he took me for a thief, a poacher, or something worse, he was still good enough to guide me to my destination, trying hard, as he led the way, to reform my defective morals ! "

.   .   .   .   .

But all that night, up to the latest hour, there was no sign of Gabrielle. She had indeed mysteriously disappeared.

CHAPTER XV.

OLD FRIENDS.

" When true friends meet in adverse hour,
  'Tis like a sunbeam through a shower—
  A watery ray an instant seen,
  The darkly closing clouds between."

Scott.

FATHER GARTHWAITE and his vistor
had not met for a good many years,
though in their younger days they had been
constant companions and bosom friends. The
meeting, though not unexpected, brought a
host of surprises to both ; for who, after years
of separation, can retain in the mind anything like an accurate impression of a former
friend ? It is not only that the features
change—this, though the most apparant, is
the least of the alterations that time works
in us—but our minds and characters, obeying
the natural laws of our existence, are undergoing a constant development of change.

How often does a man sustain a sharp shock when, coming accidentally upon some old letters or a forgotten diary, he sees for the first time the immense distance which separates his former from his present self. If our mental and moral growth can be so distinctly marked off in our own minds, how much greater must the contrast between the present and the past appear to those who have not been by to watch the changes which circumstances have wrought in us ?

There must, indeed, be something strong in the character and good in the men when an old friendship, long dormant, can be suddenly revived with all its old warmth. Even parent and child meet, after a long separation, with a certain sense of strangeness, almost of embarrassment ; and time is required to rub down the rough angles which they have acquired, and to bring them back to the old mutual adaptability—if, indeed, they can ever again be so thoroughly attuned to each other as they were before they parted.

As the two old friends sat together that

evening in the priest's study, each spent a
fruitful silence in mentally comparing present
impressions and appearances with the recol-
lections of the past. It was pleasant to
notice in each other the little traits of habit
and manner which vividly brought back the
old times when they were fellow-students in
a French *lycée.*

It was pleasant also, even though it
was tinged with sadness, to observe the
unexpected outgrowths of a new and firmer
texture in each other's nature and disposition, which made the reality of each so
like in the block, and yet so different in
detail, from the ideal which the other had
formed of it.

At last Father Garthwaite broke the
somewhat lengthened silence.

"Charles Duromme," he began, extending
his hand once more to his visitor, and uttering
the name tenderly, as though there were a
delicate enjoyment in the very sound: "I
shall continue to call you by that name, for
I know the good reason your father had for

adopting it when he was forced to become what is termed a mere business man."

" Thanks, friend Garthwaite, thanks. Your heart is still in the right place."

Then Father Garthwaite went on—" I little thought when we parted last that it would be so long before we met again. But I do not know that I altogether regret our long separation ; it adds to the pleasure of our meeting."

" Yes ; for it makes it the resurrection of a buried friendship," returned Duromme, as he warmly pressed the outstretched hand, " But how has the world dealt with you all this time ? Are you still deep in your old schemes of universal philanthropy ? "

" Nay," replied the priest, with a smile, "it is rather you who should tell me what your life has been. What can a poor persecuted priest, with a limited flock and no experiences outside his own small valley, have to say that can interest a man of the world and a soldier ? "

" A soldier," repeated Duromme with surprise. " Ah, I remember—that was my poor father's pet scheme ; he was to grind away and fill the family chest, while I was to take arms and find rank and glory to adorn the family name. But you know I never had much taste for glory of that sort, and when my father died I could not resist the old fascination which finance always had for me ever since I first began to understand my father's banking business."

" You do not mean to say that you became a banker yourself ? "

" Indeed I do. Your gold notes and bills, your stocks and shares, are, it is true, but the counters with which men play out the good or bad that is in them ; but how great the influence they exercise—what a potent engine they are for setting the world's machinery in motion ! "

" Yes," replied the priest. " But surely the power of money is more for evil than for good ? Does not all experience teach us that ? "

" Well, I do not know. It strikes me that

that is rather a narrow view. Circumstance and opportunity have a far greater share in moulding our lives than either money or sentiment, and the lives of the saints give you ample proof that it is often a mere accident which determines whether a man shall be the greatest of saints or the rankest of sinners."

Father Garthwaite looked troubled. Yet he knew that his friend was right.

"If these," he remarked, "are the views which spring from a close and intimate acquaintance with the great world, Heaven keep me from much contact with it. It is but a free-and-easy philosophy which sees only accident and blind chance in events which have moved the world. I would rather look for my causes to the finger of God."

After a pause the priest went on, "Your father's death, then, is not recent? I should have thought he was destined for a long and a happy life."

"No, my friend," replied the Frenchman in a mournful tone. "My poor old father

went off quite suddenly seventeen years ago.
He never recovered from the shock which
my sister's marriage gave him."

" Your sister? Ah; I remember—a slight,
graceful girl, who used to seem too delicate
and fragile for this rough world."

" Yes," continued Duromme; " and though
the promise of childhood is seldom realised in
after life, it was borne out in poor Marie, for
she grew up as delicate as she bade fair to be
when you knew her in short frocks. She
was like a little Dresden shepherdess, won-
drous in its prettiness, but easily upset and
shattered to atoms."

" You say she married, and matrimony is
often the best cure for feeble health. I
trust she is stronger now ? "

" Garthwaite," replied Duromme, with
sudden energy and a husky voice, " as
heaven is my witness, I know not whether
whether she be alive or dead. None of us
have known for more than seventeen long
years. And my poor father—my God, it was
cruel—he so loved her."

Father Garthwaite sat silent for a few moments, sorry that he should unconsciously have awakened an acute grief. Then he said, "If it would lighten your heart of a painful memory, give me your confidence, my friend. You know I do not ask to gratify an idle curiosity."

Duromme looked up with a new expression, almost of eagerness, in his face.

"I have nothing to conceal; but I did not mean to weary you with a miserable story, a story of my own family. You may perhaps help me in as difficult a search as ever a man had to make. You only remember my sister as a child, when she was pretty enough; but her beauty grew lustrous as she reached womanhood, and she was as good as she was handsome."

"Ah, yes," said the priest, interrupting. "It is one of the mysterious dispensations of Providence that women often are made both pretty and good—so different from men. Perhaps it is a compensation for what in them we call intellectual weakness, or rather, for the absence of intellectual strength!"

And Father Garthwaite, easily losing himself in a speculative abstraction, gazed inquiringly across at his companion.

But the Frenchman was too full of the subject to be easily led from it.

"Poor Marie, certainly," said Duromme, "was not strong-minded, or she never would have been induced to run away with a bad-hearted Scotchman.

And here Duromme brought his clenched hand down upon the table with a force which made the teacups dance, and brought a sudden nervous start from the priest.

"Who was the Englishman or Scotchman?" asked Father Garthwaite; "and why do you call him ill names?"

"Because he was a liar and a cheat!" warmly replied the banker. "He wormed himself into my sister's heart, and into the goodwill of us all, by lying tales which ought to have choked him, and by chicanery that ought to have cost him his disgraceful life!"

"Dear, dear," said the priest. "How greatly men alter! Surely this wrathful Frenchman, so broad-shouldered and so loud-voiced, can hardly be the slim and gentle friend I thought I knew so well years ago?"

Duromme's frown relaxed into a smile, and he replied, "Ah, well, as you English say, my bark is worse than my bite. But is it not enough to vex a saint? Remember you how happy we all were at our home in France, and think what a change this Scottish reptile made! He came, professing to be a man of family and of fortune, who had served with distinction in your battles, and his frank and manly air and handsome face soon touched my poor sister's heart."

Here the Frenchman dashed away a tear that hung on his dark eyelash.

"We all saw what was going on, and we approved, for a better matched couple, in all seeming, you would not find in the longest day's march. This promising son — this charming husband for our poor Marie—had indeed come of a good family, and had served as a soldier; but, after a brief career of extravagance and debauchery, he had been disgraced and expelled his country."

Father Garthwaite was perplexed. "I do not yet understand it," he began, "for though you have good reason for anger, I do not see how this accounts for your sister's disappearance. The engagement was broken off, of course, and there was an end to all acquaintance with a man unworthy of your friendship."

"Unfortunately no," replied the banker. "Of course, we would have no more to say to him. Our door was at once closed in his face, and Marie was sent away to a convent in the South, of which her own aunt was Superior, for a few months' rest and quiet. But unhappily this cheat and blackleg found out the place to which she had been sent, found means of seeing her, persuaded the poor girl that he was a hero and martyr, and induced her to run away with him and get married. Ah, my friend, I could shoot that man quite calmly."

"I am not quite sure that a moderate desire, in such a case, to inflict personal chastisement would not be even laudable," Father Garthwaite remarked, after a brief reflection. "But it is certainly wrong to wish to kill. Vengeance is not punishment."

"But the man had gone, and left no trace," returned Duromme; "and from that day to this we have never seen or heard anything at all of my poor sister."

"You have not yet told me the name of the betrayer?"

"He called himself Douglas—George Frederick Douglas—but I don't believe that was his real name. My father never recovered the blow, and after his death I carried on the search which he had commenced to find my poor sister's hiding-place, but always without success. And I am still pursuing it, and shall do so till I die, for she may be in misery and want; and, besides, I owe it to my father's memory to carry to her his loving forgiveness."

"And I will heartily do all I can to help

you," said Father Garthwaite; "but after so long an interval we must not be too sanguine of success."

"For the present," continued the visitor, "I will, with your leave, remain your guest. I want a few weeks of that perfect quiet which this lovely spot seems made for giving."

"I need not tell you how thoroughly welcome you are," replied the priest; for though I have many acquaintances here, I have few friends. I hope you have not lost your old skill over the chess-board, as I never find a good antagonist now. I play sometimes with a young artist here; but, between ourselves, he is only a drawing-room player, to whom I can comfortably give a rook."

And the eyes of the priest glistened with a pardonable appreciation of his own superiority in chess generalship.

A couple of hours later the priest and his visitor, losing all note of time, and oblivious of everything save the few boxwood and ebony toys spread out before them, were wholly absorbed in a desperate struggle to secure and to prevent the queening of an ambitious pawn which had sprung from the ranks and gone through a host of perils, only to be content in the end with royalty or death.

CHAPTER XVI.

MORE WONDER.

" All wonder is the effect of novelty upon ignorance."
—*Johnson.*

"Nature often enshrines gallant and noble hearts in weak bosoms."—*Charles Dickens.*

THE search for Gabrielle was fruitless. She had disappeared as if she had never been. The only clue that had been found was slight indeed. M'Vulcan and Mucklewut had, on the night of the mysterious disappearance of the young lady, been returning from their revels at Luckie M'Mutchkin's when they saw a boat put off to Pilot Park's schooner, which lay in the offing; and all at once the anchor was weighed, sails spread, and the schooner scudded swiftly across the Firth.

But as Park's schooner was ever moving

backwards and forwards in the Firth, little importance was attached to the fact of her departure on that particular night.

Yet Lord Charles Montgomery—whose feelings in the circumstances may, as the newspaper reporters say, be more easily imagined than described—did attach importance to the fact. With the permission of his father and Lady Kennedy, he organised a party to go in search of Gabrielle. The members of the proposed expedition consisted of himself, Guy Gordon, and Jean Graham.

But before their departure—the time of which had been kept a profound secret—a circumstance occurred which rendered Gabrielle's mysterious disappearance still more mysterious. A day or two after that sad disappearance young Tom Marling, finding the Doon was completely frozen over, determined to have an afternoon's skating. And he prevailed on his father and mother to accompany him, although they went more for Tom's safety than their feelings in other circumstances would have warranted.

A large circular hole had been cut with a saw to enable copious supplies of water to be drawn for a dyer's shed which was close at hand, and as the hole had been cut on the inner edge of a rather sharp curve which the river made at this point, the natural danger of such a break in the ice was greatly increased.

"There ought to be a rope flung across that place."

This observation, made in a low musical voice, was found to proceed from Father Garthwaite, who, with his breviary in his hand, had come there unperceived.

"A cold bath in this weather would be bad enough, but to die in such a hole— to beat one's life out in a hopeless struggle against this rigid crust of ice—ah, that would be terrible!" added the good-hearted priest.

Mr Godfrey Marling's imagination was not so easily excited. He thought the priest, with all his reputation for goodness and piety, had very little courage; and every man knows that the presence of all the other virtues will not save the supposed want of brute courage from being simply contemptible.

Besides, Father Garthwaite's naturally pale face had actually gone a shade paler at the picture which his own imagination had drawn—a proof that the race of priests had sadly degenerated since the recent age of martyrdom!

"It is not a bad idea—that about the rope," said Mr Marling, after a pause. "I think we must have one placed there."

And accordingly a long, stout rope was procured, and while one end was secured around the trunk of a tree which grew on the river bank, the other was thickly knotted and thrown slackly across the gap in the ice.

But all at once the group was interrupted by a terrible scream, and in a moment there was such a commotion and such a universal rush towards one point that the ice quivered and groaned and cracked, and seemed on the point of splitting up.

Tom Marling's luckless skates had carried

him right into the dangerous hole, and he had disappeared under the ice.

Mr Godfrey Marling, as soon as he understood what had happened, rushed to the spot, and would have gone in headlong had he not been restrained by a powerful pair of arms which lifted him off his feet, and with an easy swing pushed him several yards away.

" His head is not cool enough for this ; besides, he has a wife," said the owner of the thin, long, muscular arms. " Now, men, for God's sake, keep away ! The ice is already cracking with your weight."

There was an immediate rush to the precipitous bank.

" Don't all of you go ; six or eight of the strongest must stay here to help me ; and Father Garthwaite seized the loose end of the rope and hastily tied it round his body.

" Does anybody know which way the tide is running ?   Come, quick !"

Nobody knew.

" Has anybody a piece of paper or anything that will float ?"

While a hundred hands dived into a hundred pockets and hastily brought out penknives, bunches of keys, coins, and all sorts of miscellaneous articles warranted to sink, one of the men remaining near the hole picked up the breviary which had been dropped upon the ice when the priest seized Mr Marling.

"Will this do, Father?"

Father Garthwaite hurriedly opened the proffered volume, and with nervous shaking fingers tore out several leaves, which he threw lightly upon the cold black water.

"Thank God, there is little or no current," exclaimed the priest. "Now, my lads, when I have been under the ice half a minute, pull me out as quickly as you can. Whatever good I can do I must do in that time—I shall doubtless be insensible afterwards. Give me a full half minute, and if you can break away more of the ice and enlarge the hole, so much the better. Good-bye, and God bless you all! Pray that we may both come back alive;" and as he spoke he plunged into the water in the direction in which it was running.

It takes a long time to tell, yet in action all this was inconceivably rapid. But with what a torturing slowness did the following thirty seconds pass! The father of the poor boy whose life was in such peril ground his heel into the ice, and set his teeth in an intensity of anguish. The mother—catching, poor soul! at the priest's last words—sank upon her knees to pray; but the distraction of that fearful time was too great—no prayers would come to relieve the agonised heart. Men held their breath, women forgot to scream—the excitement was too deep for anything but painfully-deep silence.

The rope was soon hauled in, though not without difficulty; but when it was found that the boy had been recovered, the pent up feelings of the spectators were let loose, and the two insensible figures were landed on the ice in the midst of a Babel of excited tongues.

The poor lad had fortunately been carried only a yard or two from the spot where he fell in, and when the priest felt the object for which he had risked his own life he locked his arms tightly round it, and quickly lapsed into complete unconsciousness himself.

Father Garthwaite, whose immersion had been so much the shorter of the two, was soon brought round, but Tom Marling was almost given up for dead, so obstinately did the poor frozen body refuse all signs of re-animation. At last, some hours of careful effort were rewarded with success, and the lad slowly and painfully groped his way back to life.

Clutched firmly in the boy's right hand, which for a considerable time could not be opened, was the silver crucifix that had formerly belonged to Gabrielle Stuart!

CHAPTER XVII.

LADY ISLE.

"Hell, their fit habitation, fraught with fire
Unquenchable, the house of woe and pain."
Milton.

"For danger levels man and brute,
And all are fellows in their need."
Byron.

THE town of Ayr and its neighbourhood
formed a perfect nest of superstition.
Sentiment, as a rule, took the place of intellect, and, quite naturally, error was the result,
as it ever is in such circumstances.

There was a certain fairy knoll near
Greenan, where at a certain season of each
year had been heard myriads of thin, small
voices, mingled with the rustle of riding-gear.
Even Gabrielle and Charles had, with something like fear, heard the fairy sounds; but
when the lovers made minute investigation

they found that the mysterious noises were produced by withered broom-pods rattling and rustling under a fitful breeze !

There was a hirpling old woman in the village—Effie Steenson, the short for Stevenson—whose main source of living was in going round the parish nursing the sick, or washing and streiking the dead. The old woman, in the shape of a hare, had been met one night by a farmer, and he shot her in the haunch ; hence the old body's lameness !

M'Vulcan, the blacksmith, did a good trade in old horse shoes, which he carefully nailed on doors, and surmounted with branches of rowan tree, so that the devil might be kept away !

The Weeping Lady had, for the first time, been seen on the Lady Isle, much to the astonishment and alarm of the domestics.

When a Roman Catholic passed a Protestant's door, he (the former) crossed himself piously, the sacred sign being made with a piece of rowan.

Should a diseased person drop a pebble

into Mungo's Well he dropped the disease along with it.

At the top of a hill four lairds' lands met, and there at midnight the suicide was buried with a wooden stake through his or her body. In one case the miserable person had been a dreadful blasphemer, and as he was being carried to the terrible place of interment the at first heavy load became all at once as light as straw! Satan, to whom the poor wretch had sold himself, had claimed him before burial.

Out of all these superstitions have sprung Doubt; out of Doubt, Unbelief; out of Unbelief that miserable thing called Atheism.

Would it not be well if we could now begin at the other end of the stick of superstition, and deal with Atheists as we were wont to deal with witches?

Ah me! the elder Pliny put it well when he said, "There is nothing certain but that nothing is certain, and nothing prouder and more miserable than man."

There is, indeed, very much that cannot be

found out "by searching." Sometimes the
more one searches he is, in the end, much
more in the dark than when he began.

> " On this ocean's troubled breast
> Pirate bands my bark infest;
> Here the foe and there the wave,
> Death and trouble round me rave.
> Come, good Helmsman, come at last,
> Smooth the sea, and hush the blast,
> Bid these pirates turn and flee ;
> Bring to port my bark and me."

> " Barren fig-tree sure am I ;
> Every branch is bare and dry.
> Hew and burn—it merits all—
> Justly would the sentence fall,
> Yet one other year, oh spare ;
> Dig it, dung it, it may bear;
> If not, then the fire, ah me !
> Must consume the fruitless tree."

Reader, don't fancy that I am off at a
tangent. You will find, should you bear
with me long enough, that every digression
I make has something to do with the thread
which I am attempting to unravel.

Doubtless my romance may, like the
fruitless fig-tree, be "bare and dry;" but I

do not wish it consumed as yet. Spare it,
then, if not for a year, for at least a short
time. By digging and dunging, "it may
bear."

.   .   .   .   .

Turn we now for a brief period to Lord
Kennedy and some of his doings at Lady
Isle, that beautiful little spot in the Firth
of Clyde that he had turned into a small
Pandemonium. Day by day, night after
night, the place was a never-ending scene
of horrible dissipation, dreadful debauchery,
and foul cruelty.

We shall begin with one night shortly
after the incidents just recorded in our story.
In a great hall, the floor of which was
composed of huge slabs of stone, sat Lord
Kennedy and his now particular associate,
the Glasgow apothecary—an Irishman named
Dennis Burke, whose great-grandson many
years afterwards became the chief actor in
the many diabolical murders perpetrated by
the now infamous couple, so well known as
Burke and Hare.

Lord Kennedy had indeed received terrible injuries in that dreadful tourney at Glasgow. He much more resembled a wild beast than a human being. A mass of knotted hair— evidently unkempt for many months—fell loosely over his deformed features, for the blow that he had received had so fearfully disfigured him that there was hardly one recognisable part of his face to be discerned. Most men, possibly, would have preferred death at the time rather than life under such deplorable circumstances.

Public gossip had not been very far wrong. No wonder, indeed, that superstition had come in to assist rumour in the impression that the Evil One had given his assistance in the case of Lord Kennedy. His appearance was fiendish in the extreme.

His companion, Dennis Burke, was in another way quite as evil-looking. About sixty sinful summers had passed over his un-hallowed head, and many more than sixty foul crimes had made him the most hardened villain that Glasgow had ever produced.

On the back of the tall chair on which Lord Kennedy sat was perched a raven, black as is supposed to be his Satanic Majesty himself, and as evil-looking as the Evil One could possibly be painted.

"Come on, Beelzebub," said Lord Kennedy to the raven; "shout out a ribald song! And thou, blackguard Burke, see that thou joinest heartily in the chorus, or I'll scald thee to death in boiling wine."

And the raven croaked an obscene song, the refrain being chanted, in a voice no sweeter than that of the raven, by Dennis Burke.

"Well done, Beelzebub; well done, Dennis!" shouted Lord Kennedy, or all that remained of him. "Now, pile up the fire with faggots. We'll have roast Bishop for supper to-night. Ha, ha! fill up the fire with faggots."

And the raven croaked—"Burke, blackguard Burke, pile up the fire with faggots! We'll have roast Bishop for supper to-night."

And now a pause took place, while his

Lordship called for more wine, which he drank in great gulps. It was plain that he was imbibing Dutch courage by the quart. He had something on his mind, and it required wine to get rid of his mental burden.

" Hast got the young French filly safe, blackguard Burke ? Hast got her safe, I say ? " And Lord Kennedy made the measures dance as he furiously smote the strong table.

Dennis Burke grinned a horrible affirmation as he chuckled and rubbed his long, yellow, dirty hands.

" That's right, that's right, blackguard Burke ; the Devil will reward thee."

" The Devil will reward thee," croaked the dreadful raven.

" Never mind, Dennis ; let her eat her head off for the nonce. One at a time's good fishing. We'll have the Bishop first. What, ho ! without there ! bring in the Bishop ; and with him bring more wine !"

Slowly there entered, his hands bound fast

behind him, an aged man, whose shaven crown and general mein declared him to be an ecclesiastic. He bowed his head upon his breast, but spoke not.

"Come nearer to the fire, Bishop; come nearer to the fire; thou must be cold," said the brutal Kennedy.

" Thanks, my Lord, for your kind proffer; but my heavenly Master keeps me warm," meekly replied the Bishop of Ayr, for such had been the rank of the venerable-looking man.

" He does!" sneered Kennedy; "perhaps I'll keep thee warmer."

And blackguard Burke chuckled, and old Beelzebub croaked, both evidently overjoyed with the meeting.

" Bird of evil," shouted Kennedy, " bring out thy catechism and make the Bishop answer his questions. And see that thou donnest thy clerical garb."

Hopping to a corner the raven brought forth a tiny cloak and a toy mitre, with which it adroitly clothed itself, much to the delight of Lord Kennedy and Dennis Burke. Then the raven, standing on one leg, took up a little black book and pretended to read from it.

In other circumstances the effect would have been ludicrous in the extreme. But, as it was, there was something devilish in the foul bird's appearance.

"Where are the deeds? where are the deeds? where are the deeds?" croaked the raven.

But the Bishop made no sign either by word or act.

"Hearest thou, false priest? Where are the title deeds of my lands of Dunure?"

"The deeds I received in sacred trust for one who is near and ought to be dear to thee. Moreover, the lands are not thine."

"We shall see; we shall see. Dennis, Dennis, kindly give the good Bishop a seat by the fire. And, that he may not fall from his seat, bind him to it."

Soon the hoary-headed Bishop was bound to a settle, and placed in front of the now

roaring fire, where in a brief space he began
to suffer much pain.

"Now, false priest, wilt thou save thy
wretched life by divulging where are the
deeds?"

"Thou hast had mine answer," groaned the
now evidently agonised Bishop. "No fire
can extort confession from me."

"Then at once do thy duty, Dennis Burke,"
shouted Lord Kennedy.

And, with the assistance of a serving-man,
Dennis Burke threw the already seemingly
insensible ecclesiastic into the heart of the
fierce flames. In about as short a time as it
has taken to record the fact—for the story
really has foundation on fact—the good
Bishop of Ayr had evidently got rid of all
earthly troubles.

．　　　．　　　．　　　．　　　．

Suddenly a vivid flash of lightning lit up
the hall, while the crash of thunder that
immediately followed shook the strong old
building to its very foundations.

Lord Kennedy and Dennis Burke assumed

an air of indifference, but it was evident that
it was only assumed. The serving-man
tremblingly exclaimed, "This is awful!" But
the demon raven merely flapped its wings,
and croaked :

"We'll have roast Bishop for supper; we'll
have roast Bishop for supper!"

But the foul bird had reckoned too hastily.
When minute search was made not a vestige
of the remains of the Bishop was found. His
body had disappeared as completely as if it
never had been!

How could this mysterious disappearance
have come about? Even the skilled apothecary, who had seen death in most of its varied
forms, seemed to be bitterly nonplussed. He
shook his head in silent amazement as the
search went on; and grey morning had
dawned on the island ere the fruitless exam-
ination of the now cold embers was given up.

The apothecary knew more than his master.
But still he sagely shook his head in silent
amazement.

Next night the orgies were not of so noisy or hilarious a character. The mysterious disappearance of the Bishop's remains, even to the very smallest fragment, had cast a superstitious awe over Lord Kennedy and his satellite Burke; while even the raven sat on its perch, ruffling its feathers and moping.

It is ever thus with the small minds of cowards. (I even include the raven, for he appeared to have the most courage of the three.) They cannot think beyond their very limited knowledge. The footprint in the sand brings them to a sudden halt. It is too much for their poor intelligence. Besides, the cruel man, as well as the bully, is ever a coward. Cruelty and cowardice go hand in hand. They are twin brothers.

" We must wake ourselves up, blackguard Burke! Come on, old Beelzebub, give us a stave, or we'll die of *ennui*."

" We'll have roast Bishop for supper to-night," said the raven.

" We shall not, thou prating bird of evil.

Have a care, have a care! or perhaps we may
have roast raven."

"Where are the deeds? where are the
deeds?" said the raven.

"The foul fiend take thee back to hell,
whence thou camest!" and the enraged
nobleman threw the contents of his wine cup
over the too well-trained bird.

The mortified raven at once mounted to its
highest perch, and, after the fashion of its
kind, resented the personal affront by saying
not one word more.

. . . . .

Meanwhile, it ought to be explained that
our heroine Gabrielle was confined in a room
of the tall tower at Lady Isle. She had
been, by order of Lord Kennedy, carried off
when on her way to Greyscaur to visit
little Willie.

Over her head had been cast a plaid, which
kept her from screaming, and all that she
could do while being carried along the banks
of the Doon towards the sea was to unfasten
her silver crucifix and throw it on the ice—

the result being, however, that it fell through
the hole made for the purposes of a local
water supply. But the slight clue that had
been accidentally lost at the bottom of the
river was providentially found by the drown-
ing Tom Marling.

Lord Kennedy had intended to work on
the Bishop's feelings by threatening to
murder Gabrielle if he gave not up the
deeds of a certain property, which he knew
had been lodged with the Bishop for our
heroine's future benefit. But his rage had
overcome his discretion, and now the Bishop
was beyond recall.

"Curses on all concerned!" Lord Kennedy
exclaimed through his firmly-clenched teeth.
"What ho, there! Tell Pilot Park to bring
hither his wretched charge. She alone it is
who brought disaster upon me, and made me
the hideous deformity I now am."

Soon Park entered, leading the unhappy
Gabrielle Stuart; and he did so as tenderly
as his rough sailor fashion would permit.
Sorely Gabrielle shuddered, as she saw for

the first time the maimed features of Lord Kennedy.

"Aye, well may'st thou shudder, thou worthy descendant of the woman who brought eternal punishment on mankind. See what thou hast accomplished!"

And he threw back the matted locks that nearly concealed his countenance, and discovered a face of the most diabolical character.

"My Lord," said Gabrielle, meekly, "what have I in common with your sad misfortunes? Thou art mistaken, my good Lord. I am an innocent and assuredly a helpless girl."

"Innocent!" he hissed; "no woman on earth was ever innocent; not from the dawn of creation. Helpless! no woman on earth is helpless; she hath ever the deceit of a serpent and the talons of a tigress!"

Then the tears rose to Gabrielle's lovely eyes as she said, "Would to the Blessed Virgin that I had never been born!"

"Make not unavailing regrets about having been born. Soon thou shalt die. I have arranged it."

With maidenly dignity, and without the slightest sign of fear, Gabrielle said, "The Lord giveth, and the Lord taketh away; blessed be the name of the Lord."

"Now, hark thee, Park. With all haste have this brazen hussy sewn up in a sack, and drop her in the Firth. I'll no more of her."

Still more dignified than before—in fact with a spark of indignation—the maiden uttered, "*En Dieu est ma fiance!*"

Lord Kennedy's eyes sparkled with almost unwonted fury as he heard the well-known sentence ; but his fury was suddenly turned to fear at the sight he presently saw.

Standing in the huge fire-place, and as if in the heart of the flames, appeared the Bishop of Ayr, who had on the previous night been so inhumanly burned.

"Where are the deeds ? where are the deeds ?" shouted the raven from his perch.

"Thou hast spoken well, maiden," said the Bishop in a hollow voice ; "put thy trust in God." And the form vanished.

Lord Kennedy swooned, and fell back in his chair. When he returned to consciousness he found that Pilot Park and Gabrielle had disappeared. Dennis Burke lay apparently insensible on the floor, and the foul raven was croaking, "We'll have roast Bishop for supper; we'll have roast Bishop for supper."

"Search the Castle,"shouted Lord Kennedy, "and let no one leave the island to-night. Treachery; I say, without there, treachery!"

And a thorough search was made, high and low, in every nook and cranny of the Castle, and all over the little island.

But the birds had flown. Park's schooner was discerned dancing over the waves, and going in the direction of the Arran Hills. She would soon be completely out of sight, as already she was far beyond capture.

Pilot Park had long and faithfully served his lord and master in various ways. But he "drew the line" at actual crime. He resolutely refused to harm a hair of Gabrielle's head. He had not even known what was his mission when his vessel had been ordered to

be off the mouth of the Doon on the night of
the young lady's forcible seizure.

Moreover, from a Platonic point of view,
Park was ever under the strange spell of
Gabrielle's presence—a spell which our hero,
Charles Montgomery, had thus immortalised
from another point of view :—

THE ENCHANTRESS.

Where lurks the power, Enchantress tell,
That binds me with its potent spell,
And swift as lightning from above,
Hath fired my soul with flames of love?

What magic dwells within that face,
What witch'ry in that queenly grace!
Why lives in each fond look and tone
A charm that you possess alone?

Hath Cupid, in a wanton hour,
To thee resigned his godlike power,
To thee assigned the fatal dart
That straightway cleaves the captive heart?

If so, thy might doth his excel,
For thou canst strike and cure as well;
While he, with all his art and skill,
Can do no more than wound or kill.

Park had undertaken to bring a cargo of wine from Bordeaux, and, putting all the circumstances before her, Gabrielle, for her own personal safety, agreed to ship to France with the sailor, whose own cabin was entirely given up to her use. And a very far from uncomfortable place the cabin was.

There were, indeed, few luxuries to be found in the cabin of such a small vessel; but there were comforts not a few. And in her position even discomfort was far preferable to death or dishonour.

Some there may be who will set down Gabrielle's decision as rash, if not even dangerous. But she had barely a choice in the matter. To have gone back to Greenan was to have gone back to destruction, for Lord Kennedy was the most vindictive of mortals, and his rage for a time would be most ungovernable. Poor Gabrielle was indeed sorely afraid that some act of cruelty would, in the circumstances, be perpetrated on the good Lady Kennedy.

Moreover, the maiden, some days before,

had been told by Lady Kennedy a considerable part of her strange antecedents.

Behold, then, the weeping Gabrielle fast on her way over the sea to her native France. Yet she continued prayerfully to repeat, *"En Dieu est ma fiance!"*

CHAPTER XVIII.

A MOTHER'S GRATITUDE.

" Bright as his manly sire the son shall be
 In form and soul, but, ah! more blest than he.
 Thy fame, thy worth, thy filial love, at last,
 Shall soothe this aching heart for all the past!"

Campbell.

" And yet believe me, good as well as ill,
 Woman's at best a contradiction still.
 Heaven, when it strives to polish all it can
 Its last best works, forms but a softer man."

Pope.

I AM much afraid that a mother's love and a mother's care are not always or altogether requited as they ought to be by her children. It sadly seems to me that now-a-days boys, like the offspring of inferior animals, go off on their own account as soon as they find they are able to do so, leaving their parents to the usually far from tender mercies of old age, and, it may be, disease.

Some sons there may be, indeed, who have been sent off to seek their living at a too early age, and who have never earned success; but there are many—alas, too many!—who, as soon as they get the Atlantic or the Pacific between them and their parents, seem to forget that such persons ever lived.

The peasantry of France, for example— as I have stated in a former chapter—are remarkably kind to their children; but as soon as the youngsters begin to get married the parents are relegated to the stable loft, or it may be the barn, in which to end their miserable existence.

Surely our own much-beloved country is not coming to this! Is filial affection on the wane in Scotland? Can it be that the civilising influences of education are causing us to make a retrograde movement? Our lucky stars forfend that, when "everybody" is educated, the exceptions to the rule—the poor wretched few who are bound to know absolutely nothing—will be sought out and looked upon with as much admiring reverence as we did not long ago upon Thomas Carlyle!

Reader, pardon the disgression. I now hark back to the afternoon when Tom Marling was rescued from the river Doon by Father Garthwaite—both, as I have already remarked, having been in a state of insensibility.

The sufferers had been removed at once to the nearest cottage, where the work of resuscitation was carried on. When Tom was sufficiently restored to bear removal, Father Garthwaite, who had first returned to consciousness, suddenly remembered that he had lost his breviary; and when the remains of that volume were handed to him he was sadly perplexed and grieved on seeing what havoc he had hastily made among its pages.

"I have been guilty of waste—wilful waste!" he cried, in energetic self-accusation. "I have spoiled my good old book—such an old friend, too!"

"Come, come," said Dr Turner—the parish

leech—who had hastened to the spot in the hope that he might be useful when he first heard of the accident. "This is scarcely worthy of you, Mr Garthwaite. You have saved the boy's life — surely that far more than balances the loss of a prayer-book?"

Father Garthwaite looked at the vicar with amazement.

"Can anything excuse waste? I might have torn out the fly-leaf without injury to the text, or I might have taken an old letter or any odd scrap—see, I have plenty in my pocket—to have found out which way the river ran. But I was always apt to be too hasty when I had most need of mature reflection;" and the poor priest sighed dolorously.

"Yes, and mature reflection would have drowned the boy. I had no idea that you held human life so cheap."

Dr Turner's tone was bitter and sarcastic. He could not understand this pitiful reference to trivial details after such an exploit as the priest had performed.

"Nay, you do me great wrong, sir," replied Father Garthwaite with dignity, as he hastily tossed the long thin hair from his broad temples. "I hold life to be more precious than all the books in the universe. But here we have no such question—the life has been saved, and I still think it could have been saved without the wanton destruction of my breviary."

"A breviary!" retorted the other; "and what about a wretched breviary, that it should be mourned as if it were God's Holy Word?"

"Nay," said the priest, calmly, "I but deplored the waste. And yet my breviary contains many of the great truths of revealed religion."

"Nothing short of the Bible itself contains the Almighty's great truths, penned by His own hand. I well know that the priests of your persuasion keep back as much as possible the Bible from the people. But it is wrong, very wrong."

And the learned leech—as all Scotch

Protestants did then, do now, and are likely to do to the end of the chapter—waxed theologically indignant, and metaphorically "cock'd his beaver."

"Ah, but only think, my good friend," quietly said the priest, "that when even the learned have much difficulty in understanding many passages of the Book, how must it be with the ignorant? Better, surely, that their spiritual leaders should explain the Word to them."

"Let every man make his own explanation," retorted the doctor doggedly. "Then look at the mummeries and genuflections enjoined by the Romish Church."

"Aye, aye, my good friend; but did not David, the son of Jesse, even dance before the Lord?"

"Doubtless, doubtless; and David and his followers at the same time held sweet-scented phials in their hands. Are we to worship Heaven by the aid of smelling-salts?"

And the orthodox doctor waxed still more theologically indignant.

"Moreover," contended Father Garthwaite, "there are very many passages of so-called Holy Writ that are hopelessly obscure, and not believed to be of Divine inspiration. And when the body is weak, my good friend, it is the better of the support of a corselet."

"Look here, Father Garthwaite, I take the whole of the Scriptures, from the first verse of Genesis to the last verse of Revelations, to be inspired writ. I am a strong man, and require no corselet."

And the doctor at once flattered himself that he had settled the entire question, now, henceforth, and for ever.

"Well, well, my good friend, let the subject pass," said the amiable priest. "It is sad, indeed, that after nearly seventeen hundred years of religious rancour we are no nearer to Christ than ever we were. Alas, alas, that strife should prevail in the name of the Lord!"

Are we any nearer now? Very, very little. In some few respects we have retrograded.

The strife is still as strong, the rancour still as ridiculous, the clergy still almost as ignorant, and very nearly as bigoted.

Perhaps in good time the School Board will do what the Church has so long tried, but ineffectually, to accomplish.

But the conversation was interrupted by Mrs Marling, who, having seen Tom restored and apparently none the worse for his submersion, now came to thank the boy's preserver.

The poor lady's gratitude was low-voiced and faltering, for she was pained by recollecting how lightly she had often spoken and thought of the priest as a priest and a heretic, but her gratitude was not the less deep and earnest.

Father Garthwaite modestly shrank from the mingled thanks and praises that were so earnestly offered him.

"Nay, madam, your gratitude belongs to God : not to one of his humblest instruments. I have but done my duty—a duty which the barest humanity compelled—and surely but small thanks are due for that?"

This was, indeed, too true. But how many of us do our duty in such dangerous circumstances? Are the days and the deeds of chivalry departed, never to return?

And if Mrs Marling chose to consider Father Garthwaite a hero, and if this feeling were made stronger instead of weaker by the priest's humility, that was a matter lying simply between Mrs Marling and her own conscience.

A few days later, when Father Garthwaite was opening a new and splendidly-bound breviary which some anonymous friend had sent him, and wondering who could know his wants so exactly, and supply them with so handsome a gift, Mrs Marling was upon her knees, beseeching Heaven's goodness for the man who had saved her child, and offering up a supplementary prayer, after some mental disturbance, that she might be forgiven for in any way encouraging the circulation of heretical literature!

Such is human nature—more especially female human nature. Such, indeed, has always been female human nature. As we say in Scotland, "Women are kittle cattle to deal with." Doubtless they have quite as much courage as men, and it is certain they can bear greater pain ; but, but——
Well, I had better wind up this chapter.

CHAPTER XIX.

A FAMOUS SCOTTISH MARTYR.

"Avenge, O Lord, Thy slaughtered saints, whose bones
Lie scattered on the *Scottish* mountains cold.
E'en them who kept Thy truth, so pure of old,
When all our fathers worshipped stocks and stones,
Forget not: in Thy Book record their groans."

Milton.

FATHER GARTHWAITE had deeply studied the story of his friend Charles Duromme. The more he thought over it the more absorbed he became in reflection. At last he had a long interview with Duromme—an interview that lasted over two hours. The result was that Duromme requested and obtained permission to join the expedition that had been arranged for the purpose of finding Gabrielle.

During the interview each had evidently kept something to himself. In fact there had

not altogether been the want of that reserve
which generally exists in what is termed true
friendship, although it must not be inferred
that they were in anyway attempting to
deceive each other. Each evidently believed
in the then-unwritten lines of Robert Burns,

> " Aye free, off-han,' your story tell,
> When wi' a bosom crony ;
> But still keep something to yoursel',
> Ye scarcely tell to ony."

" I should fancy, from what you state, that
Gabrielle will have been carried off to
Glasgow," said Duromme thoughtfully.

" And if she be not there, I dare say we
shall soon find out her whereabouts," significantly said Father Garthwaite.

The river Doon had for many days been
dragged without effect, as young Lord Montgomery had confidently prophesied. He had
an instinctive idea that Gabrielle had been
carried off by myrmidons of Lord Kennedy,
and he fancied she would once more be found
in Glasgow. Accordingly it was settled that
the expedition should proceed to that city

without delay, and there make a thorough search.

Jean Graham, that she might ride on horseback *en cavalier*—which was then no uncommon fashion among females—was elegantly dressed as a page. And a pretty boy she looked, although, perhaps, she blushed too much to be taken for a boy.

.   .   .   .   .

At an early part of their journey the progress of the party was temporarily barred at Kilmarnock. Here Charles Montgomery found a very different state of matters from that he had experienced but a short time before. Cock-fighting had given way to men-hunting. General Dalziel — "The Bloody Dalziel," as he was called—with his murderous military, was in possession of the town.

The most barbarous atrocities were being perpetrated on those who had the temerity to adhere to the Covenant. The "Thieves' Hole," a loathesome dungeon close to the Cross, was crammed to suffocation with men

—aye, and women, too—who had dared to worship God after the faith that was in them.

In this "Thieves' Hole" the prisoners were so crowded together that, according to an account of the period, "they could not move themselves night nor day, but were obliged constantly to stand up."

In this dreadful place the wretched sufferers were enduring the most acute tortures. One poor fellow, indeed, seemed to be dying, and his friends earnestly implored the commander for his liberty.

According to Mr Archibald M'Kay's recent "History of Kilmarnock," the poor fellow was relieved "on the condition that, dead or alive, his body should be returned."

Then the account goes on, "Shortly after his release from jail death put an end to all his sorrows; but his relatives were compelled to carry his corpse back to the door of the prison, where it lay exposed to the public gaze until Dalziel was pleased to give liberty for its interment."

This was the position in which our party found Kilmarnock. Men were being hunted like foxes into cold caves and along bleak hillsides.

A small party of Dalziel's soldiers had commanded Charles Montgomery and his followers to halt.

Not being able to give, as the officer thought, a proper account of themselves, they were taken into the town, and to the outside of the house in which General Dalziel lodged. This house was situated on the east bank of the water, at the end of the Old Bridge.

From one of the windows Dalziel haughtily questioned Charles.

" Art thou on the business of the State, or how ? "

" We are on strictly private, but very urgent, business," answered Charles.

" It's nature ? "

Charles briefly explained the cause and the character of the expedition.

" Humph ! " exclaimed the General ; " if

every errant damsel were to be traced with
as much minuteness as seems to be carried
out in this case, soon every man would be in
search of every woman in the country."

"Being a free agent, I do as I choose,"
haughtily retorted Charles.

"Insolent, art thou? Let them be detained
until I find out the truth or otherwise of this
unlikely story."

Charles involuntarily drew his sword, and
he was followed in like manner by Guy
Gordon and Duromme.

But they were soon overpowered by num-
bers and disarmed.

Ultimately, however, Charles Montgomery
gave Dalziel convincing proofs as to his own
position and the *bona fides* of the party, and
they were allowed to proceed on their
unpleasant journey.

Without further adventure, the expedition
arrived in Glasgow. But it happened to be
on a most unfortunate day.

It was the sad day on which the Rev.

Donald Cargill, minister of the Barony Church, was to suffer martyrdom at the Cross of Glasgow, and the streets leading to the scaffold were crowded with spectators.*

The people were morose, and ready for an outbreak; but they were overawed by the presence of many soldiers.

After Mr Cargill had come to the scaffold— I give this on the written testimony of Guy Gordon, who was present—he stood with his back towards the ladder, fixed his eyes upon the multitude, and desired their attention. After singing a part of the cxviii. Psalm, from the 16th verse to the close, he looked up to the windows on both sides of the scaffold with a smiling countenance, requesting the people to compose themselves, and hear a few words that he had to say.

Then began the noble details of that dying testimony which still is as exciting to the

* Mr Cargill was really executed, in the year 1681, at the Cross of Edinburgh.

people of Scotland as was wont to be the sound of a war trumpet.

" This is," began Mr Cargill, "the most joyful day that ever I saw in my pilgrimage on earth ; my joy is now begun, which I see shall never be interrupted. I see both my interest, and His truth, and the sureness of the one, and the preciousness of the other."

At this point a rattle of military drums drowned Cargill's voice, when he ceased, and waited patiently until the soldiers had finished. But during his quarter of an hour's address the drums were beaten three times. After having been commanded to go up the scaffold ladder, which he did calmly and fearlessly, Cargill said—

" Farewell all relations and friends in Christ; farewell acquaintances, and all earthly enjoyments ; farewell reading and preaching, praying and believing, wanderings, reproaches, and sufferings. Welcome, Father, Son, and Holy Ghost; into Thy hands I commit my spirit."

Then he prayed a little, and, according to

the language of the period, "the executioner turned him over praying."

Thus nobly died one who bore testimony to the cruelties perpetrated on those who choose to worship God in their own way. For years he had protested against what a chronicler of the time boldly terms "vast and exorbitant fines, extorted by troops of soldiers, plundering, quartering, beating, wounding, binding men like beasts, chasing them away from their houses, compelling them, though sick, to go to church, consuming and wasting their provision with dogs, and promiscuously abusing as well those that conformed as them that refused; and if any testified their resentment at these vermin of ignorant and scandalous curates, or refused to give them their title, they were imprisoned, scourged, stigmatised, and banished to Barbadoes or other foreign parts."

.   .   .   .   .

Returning from this awful scene, Guy Gordon pointed out to Lord Charles and

Duromme that part of the green where the tournament had been held, and where Lord Kennedy had recieved his dreadful injuries.

"Would to God that the battle-axe had done its work more thoroughly! I know it was intended that it should have done so," said the Frenchman abstractedly.

Lord Charles and Guy Gordon exchanged glances. What could Duromme possibly know of the matter? That was the question each with his eyes asked the other.

Duromme quickly noticed the significant glances, and said confusedly—

"From Father Garthwaite I have had details of the encounter."

This remark simply added to the mystery. How could Father Garthwaite know that the axe was intended to do its work thoroughly? To Charles and Guy the situation became more and more inexplicable.

.   .   .   .   .

Next day Lord Charles received, by special messenger, a sealed communication from Lady Kennedy. He did not divulge all the

contents of the packet to the other members
of the party, but simply informed them that
they were to proceed at once to Dumbarton,
and take the first packet to France, to which
country Lady Kennedy believed Gabrielle
had been taken.

More mystery! How could Lady Kennedy
have such belief? From whom did she
receive her information? Moreover, sufficient
time had not elapsed for her to have received
a communication from Gabrielle.

The fact seemed to be, and it began slowly
to dawn on Guy Gordon, that Lady Kennedy
must have a paid spy at Lady Isle, but that
from its isolated position communication with
the mainland was necessarily infrequent and
very often unsafe.

According to Lady Kennedy's instructions
the party at once proceeded on their way to
Dumbarton, then the key to the Western
Highlands, and having communication with
various parts of France twice a month.

But any description of the ancient burgh
of Dumbarton must be deferred until a future

chapter. Meanwhile we shall call a halt—— as the party had to do owing to the sudden lameness of one of the horses—at the ancient, and at that time famous, town of Paisley, long celebrated as being perhaps the very centre of Scottish industry and commercial prosperity.

But, as is well known, Glasgow, the Second City in the Empire, in time took the wind out of the manufacturing sails of Paisley; although, even to this day, Paisley has no reason to be ashamed of its industrial and commercial position.

CHAPTER XX.

PAISLEY.

" At the industrious man's house Hunger looks in, but
dares not enter! Nor will the bailiff or the constable
enter, for industry pays debts."—*Franklin*.

" Arouse thee youth! it is no human call—
God's Church is leaguer'd—haste to man the wall."
James Duff.

MY readers must not fancy that I am
endeavouring to write historically, or
with anything like historical accuracy. As
far as possible, however, the general references I make to places in the West of
Scotland have been carefully gathered from
standard works.

History is at times strangely compiled.
Look, for example, at the story of "Greyfriars'
Bobby," now recorded in the archives of the
city of Edinburgh. Bobby, according to the
legend, was a dog that followed its master's

remains to Greyfriars' Kirkyard, and lay until the day of its death on his grave, only going outside occasionally to obtain food.

Now, I well know that this tale concerning "Greyfriars' Bobby" is utterly untrue, notwithstanding that a certain dog was given a gold chain by the Lord Provost of Edinburgh, and that the Baroness Burdett-Coutts raised a monument in the form of a fountain to a certain dog's memory. In a future chapter I intend to give the history of that same dog.

It always seems to me that the poor dog—for there really was a dog, but no dog that lay on its master's grave—after its investiture with the grand gold chain, died of pure shame of itself!

.   .   .   .   .

But as to Paisley. In 1488 James IV. made Paisley into a burgh. Soon after the Union the town began to flourish by reason of its manufacturing industry. It first began with plaids, checks, linen handkerchiefs, and thread. These were in time followed by the manufacture of silk gauze, in imitation of Spitalfields.

In time this trade became so successful that London had to relinquish the lead to Paisley. Companies came from the English metropolis and established themselves in Paisley, and soon the town became famous for its commerce and industrial enterprise.

Prior to the Reformation, Paisley had a rich monastery, in which the "black monks" were alleged to have had very many merry meetings. It was the black monks who wrote that curious work still in existence in London, "The Black Book of Paisley."

The ancient Abbey wall, built of cut stone, gives a good idea of the former grandeur of the place. On it there is the following inscription :—

> " Thy celsit the Abbot George of Shaw,
> About my Abbey girt mak this waw,
> An hundredth, four hundredth year.
> Eighty-four, the date but weir :
> Pray for his salvation
> That laid this noble foundation."

Paisley for poets! Then, as it is now, Paisley was famous for poets. I suppose the poetical feeling is engendered by the natural beauties of the surrounding district, which are of a very attractive character. To give some idea of the number of poets at one time in Paisley, permit me to retail a short anecdote.

The late Professor Aytoun was once invited to a banquet there. His train was late, and when he did emerge from the railway station he was accosted by one of two weavers who had been sent to hasten him.

"Are ye Maister Aytoun the poet?" was the good man's question, to which an affimative gesture was given.

"Come awa', man, come awa'; ye're unco late. There's forty o' us waitin' on ye, and we're a' poets thegither."

.   .   .   .   .

The party, headed by Lord Charles, had reached Paisley on a Saturday, which was the market day; and before they could get their broken-down horse replaced it was found prudent not to proceed further that day. On Sunday it was strictly forbidden to travel, under heavy pains and crushing penalties.

On the Saturday evening Jean Graham made an important communication to Guy Gordon. She felt assured they were being dogged. In Glasgow her quick eye had detected a little old man staring intently at them, and that evening she had seen him in Paisley. He had donned the broad-brimmed slouched hat of the period, and wore a loose cloak, with the upper part of which he could most effectually conceal the lower part of his features.

Guy immediately communicated the intelligence to Lord Charles, who pondered over it deeply for a time.

"All that we can do is," he ultimately said, "to keep a sharp look-out, and be strictly on our guard."

Sunday settled the correctness of Jean's surmises. There, opposite the windows of the hostelry at which they had put up, in

Moss Street, stood the little old man peering up at the house. Seeing that he was observed he quickly disappeared down the next street.

Of course all the members of the expedition went to afternoon service in the Abbey Church. It had been a very grand building, and was in the form of a cross. The glass of the great north window, one of the loftiest in Scotland, showed a magnificent picture of the "Taking down from the Cross." The west and north doors were richly decorated with sculpture, as were the two ranges of pointed windows.

In one of the corners of the wall was a niche containing a statue of the Virgin, with a distich under her feet:—

> " Hac ne vade viâ, nisi dixeris Ave Maria :
>   Sic semper sine væ; qui tibi dicit Ave."

Which may be freely translated—

> " Do not travel this way without supplication :
>   May he ever be happy who prays to thee."

In fact, the entire building was one of surpassing grandeur.

The service was according to the ritual of the English Church, and the preacher, reading scrupulously from a manuscript, enunciated ideas that were becoming highly unpopular throughout Scotland at the time.

He concluded his discourse by saying, "On this subject I shall say no more at present."

"Because ye canna," was shrilly shouted by a woman in the body of the kirk. "Your sermon paper is exhausted, and ye canna utter another word."

The congregation looked aghast, utterly surprised by the boldness of the woman; and for a time no one moved.

Then she continued, "Oh, for the sad defection o' ministers in puir auld Scotland! I fear me, when the Almighty makes inquisition for blood, some ministers' hands will not be found thoroughly free thereof."

The preacher had been known to be in favour of some of the recent disgraceful executions for conscience' sake.

At length two tall halberdiers pushed their

way along the aisle, and rudely seized the
greatly excited woman.

As she was taken struggling along the
stone pavement she shouted still louder,
" I enter my protestation against all the
violation done to the work o' God these
twenty years bygone. You have burnt the
Covenant made with Jehovah, and you have
thrust prelates into the Lord's house, thou
limb o' antichrist, misnamed Duke o' York."

Even outside, in the churchyard, might
be heard plainly her shouts.

" Yea, thou hast set a trap upon Mizpeh,
and spread a net upon Tabor ! "

This woman was none other than Isabel
Alison, of Perth, who afterwards suffered
martyrdom in the Grassmarket of Edinburgh.

.   .   .   .   .

The strange scene had a saddening influence upon Jean Graham, who wept bitterly.
But even worse was to come. At the conclusion of the service the clergyman requested
the congregation to retain their seats for a
few minutes. A young woman was to stand

in the "cutty-stool," and be publicly rebuked
for the crime of unchastity—a shameful exhibition that, I am sorry to be informed,
may be witnessed even at the present day
in some parts of the North of Scotland.

"Mary Morrison Manderson, stand up,"
said the clergyman.

And the trembling girl stood up before all
the congregation ; a larger one than usual
having been brought together to "enjoy"
the wretched woman's grief.

Then went on the tragical farce of
"rebuke." A frail man in the pulpit—
attempting to take the power of God from
His own hands—with comical solemnity,
rebuked a frail girl standing up in a pew !

But the worst of such a serio-comedy is
the belief that its being enacted purifies the
frail girl—purges her from sin ! And yet
we rail at confession to priests.

According to my own recollection, it is
more than twenty years since, in a certain
western town, a young women, who had
confessed to be in a certain condition, was

thus publicly rebuked. Subsequently, and of course hurriedly, she got married, but as yet the "interesting event" has not taken place.

And there, in that grand old Cathedral in Paisley, and within a few pews of the truly-wretched young woman, sat her aged father, his long grey hair going fast with sorrow to the grave. The old man leant his withered face upon his long, lean hands, while the scalding tears could be seen trickling from between his gaunt fingers.

"Why, oh, why did you take me to such a place?" sobbingly asked Jean Graham as they passed out through the churchyard.

At Greenan no "cutty-stool" event had occurred in her time; in fact, she had never heard of the disgraceful ceremony.

"Calm yourself," said Guy Gordon kindly, kissing a tear from her lovely cheek.

Looking round, Jean thought she saw the loose cloak of the little old man disappear behind a tall tombstone.

From the same direction came a rough-

looking fellow, who accosted the page with—
" Methinks thou weepest too copiously to be
a boy.   Eh, malapert ?"

" What meanest thou, clown ?" said Guy
Gordon angrily, and he laid his hand on the
hilt of his sword.

" What I say," said the stranger.   " Nay,
man, put up thy sword.   It takes two to play
at weapons, and in the end thou mightest
have by far the worst of it."

" Begone ! else I'll run thee through the
body ;" and Guy drew his sword.

"And this is my thanks," said the stranger,
sneeringly ; "this is my thanks for hinting to
this boy"—and he emphasised the word—
" that a much more severe punishment than
he has seen awarded to-day is given to
females who go to church mumming in the
garb of the male sex."

This was indeed a home-thrust that Guy
did not expect ; and as the stranger was
moving off through the crowd that had collected round them, Guy deemed it prudent
to sheath his sword, and hurry off with

Jean towards the gate of the ancient churchyard.

Fortunately, gloaming was casting its foggy
shroud over the place, or there might have
been a serious disturbance, and the entire
party suddenly arrested.

Even as it was, a storm seemed brewing
among the crowd who were rapidly "scailing"
from the kirk.

" Bonnie wark, indeed, on the Lord's-day,
and in the Lord's house, for hizzies to be
gaun about dressed in men's claes," said an
austere-looking burgher.

" Ay, and even kissin' ane anither in God's
ain consecrated ground," said a middle-aged
maiden, who evidently envied the embrace that
Guy Gordon had bestowed on Jean Graham.

" To the ducking-stool wi' the guizin' jaud,"
shouted another aged maiden.

However, Lord Charles soon poured oil on
the troubled waters. With a few kind words
and a few gold pieces he took up the attention
of the crowd until the lovers got safely out of
the churchyard.

That night Lord Charles, Duromme, and Guy Gordon had a conference, when it was resolved to leave Paisley before daylight in the morning. They were now doubly assured that their movements were being strictly watched, and that consequently they were incurring very considerable danger in remaining where they were.

Accordingly, the landlord received orders to have the horses ready at an appointed time in the morning, and next day saw our travellers in the ancient burgh of Dumbarton.

CHAPTER XXI.

FROM SCOTLAND TO FRANCE.

"In southern climes the radiant sun
A brighter light displays,
But I love best his milder beams
That shine on Scotland's braes."
Anon.

"And wither'd murder,
With Tarquin's ravishing strides, towards the design
Moves like a ghost." *Shakespeare.*

"DUMBARTON'S drums beat bonnie, O!"
Poor Douglas, Earl of Dumbarton. Thy
drums did in their time beat bonnie; but thy
fate was a hard one. Thou stuck too truly
to the Royal Scottish cause, and ended thy
days in exile. But thou hast left behind
thee an imperishable name; whilst the men
of the ancient royal burgh which gave thee
thy title have perhaps shown more martial
courage than those of any other town in
broad Scotland.

"Saw ye Rory Murphy, Rory in his tartan;
Saw ye Rory Murphy, piping through Dumbarton?"

Once the capital of a kingdom of Britons, established in the vale of the Clyde, rocky Dumbarton has a noble as well as an ancient history. It was, too, at one time, the seat of the immortal Fingal. Moreover, Boethius, the Roman statesman and philosopher, asserts that Dumbarton was possessed by the Caledonians long before the Britons, and that it resisted all the efforts of Agricola, the father-in-law of Tacitus.

Dumbarton was, indeed, the strongest fortress of its time, and was long deemed impregnable; but it was in the year 756 sorely reduced by famine, whilst it was taken by escalade in the year 1551. The Scotch thistle, which grows in great abundance in the neighbourhood of the town, had for a time, but for a time only, to meekly bend its dejected head.

. . . . .

Our travellers were fortunate in finding that a packet would sail that night for France.

That, however, they might not incur further danger by being watched, they at once arranged in town the necessary accommodation for their steeds, and went on board at once.

After a lengthened but favourable voyage, they arrived safely at the port of Calais, then held by the English. At once, following Lady Kennedy's instructions, Lord Charles proceeded to a certain hotel where he was likely to find the missing Gabrielle.

To his great annoyance and deep dismay he found that, two days before, she had proceeded to Paris, in the company of one of the female domestics of the hotel. She had gone, he was further informed, to make inquiries concerning her parentage.

Pilot Park—sailor-like in his generosity—had given Gabrielle as much gold as would pay her expenses, and had arranged a date for her return to Calais and subsequent return to Scotland.

Accordingly, there could be nothing else arranged than to follow her to the gay capital.

After a night's rest at Calais, our travellers early next morning took seats in the diligence, and were soon slowly lumbering along the road towards Lille.

Although the distance was only sixty miles, it was night ere Lille was reached. At first the novelty of the country made the journey agreeable enough, but soon the plunging of the huge Flemish horses, the jangling of their bells, and the eternal swaying to and fro of the monster vehicle itself, made the slow journey uncomfortable in the extreme.

The driver, too—Le Bœuf, who had held the reins forty years—got a little *gris*—got half-drunk, in fact—on the way; and his language to the horses, as they now and again nearly brought the whole affair to grief in a *casse-cou*, or break-neck place, was not of the most highly edifying character. "*Attendé infame!*" was about the least effusive of his horsey parlance; while his *pestes, sacres,* and *mon dieus* were more numerous than pleasing.

But when at last they did reach the hotel

at which they were to put up for the night,
every attention was shown to the tired
travellers. Madame the hostess stood herself
at the door of the *coupé* of the diligence, and
with her own hand assisted Jean Graham to
alight—Jean was now attired in the clothing
of her sex—and handed her over to Jeanette,
a pretty little maid with a white cap, from
which long white bands hung down her
slender waist.

She wore a neat bodice and a prettily
striped petticoat. Altogether Jean Graham
thought she had never seen a more charming
little woman ; she certainly had never before
seen a servant so polite and painstaking.

French servants—I mean female servants—
cannot help being polite and painstaking.
Besides, they are in the highest degree industrious.

The Franco-Prussian war caused me to
come to the sad conclusion that Frenchmen
were emasculated by the first Napoleon. And
yet in almost every peasant's house is to be
found the picture of Napoleon First or Third.

It seems to me that, had Frenchwomen been sent out to do battle for their country there would not have been a Prussian left to tell the tale.

Our youthful education, such as it was, led us to believe that a Frenchwoman was ever fair and continually false—that, in fact, she was no better than she ought to be. But experience proves that Frenchwomen, as a rule, are as industrious as they are sensible— as virtuous as they are loving.

Here at Lille is the comfortable Hotel du Louvre—landlord, Monsieur Pay, an Englishman by birth, a Frenchman by adoption— where everything in the way of creature comforts can be had in perfection.

Lille was then (when there were no railways) a busy manufacturing place, the chief town on the Chemin du Nord, and beautifully situated on the Deule. Thus it was bound to keep a good hotel.

The talkative host heralds the soup. The company, in addition to our Scotch friends, consists of three officers from the garrison, M. Boulanger, avocat, and M. le Vicaire, with M. le Chef de Police thrown in. It seems to me that no dinner can be partaken of in France without the presence of a chef de police.

And how are Messieurs the Scotch? (" Garçon, bread for Monsieur le Vicaire.") What a pity such a fine people should have abjured the Mother Church. ("Jeanette, wine for Monsieur le Chef.") Ah, poor Marie Stuart! how she was foully murdered by the gros cochon Elizabeth! ("Faquin, une grande bouteilie Volnay.") This wine, milor Ecossais, has been in bottle upwards of a quarter of a century.

And thus Monsieur Pay rattles on and bustles about, always attentive to his guests, and never above his business. Had he not been valet to the King? and had not the King first started him as a hotel-keeper at Boulogue-sur-Mer?

Being tired out with their lengthened journey, our travellers retired early to their respective rooms—Duromme leaving instructions that he should be called at an early hour, as he had business to transact in the town.

"To that which we call BED in common breath,
     The name of SEPULCHRE the Cambrians gave,
Because, as sleep itself resembles Death,
     So doth the downy couch the silent grave."

But there was something in the air that night. Lord Charles could get no repose, and the same was the case with Guy Gordon. About three in the morning each fancied he heard a stealthy footstep going along the courtyard gallery that is so common in French hotels. The watch-dog, too, had heard the sound, for he gave first a dismal howl and then a short, sharp, angry bark.

Then there came a muffled shriek of agony that caused the blood to curdle in the veins of Lord Charles. Jumping hastily from his couch, he seized his sword, and rushed out on to the wooden gallery, where he found Guy Gordon, also sword in hand.

"Heard you aught, Guy?" asked young
Montgomery in a hoarse whisper.

"The sound I heard caused my flesh to
creep.   What could it mean?"

And they peered into the darkness, but
could discern nothing.   After waiting some
time Lord Charles suggested the sound might
have been caused by the pain of some one
suffering from nightmare.   And each returned
to his chamber.

The sun was pretty high ere they awoke,
and then the awakening was caused by a
piercing scream.

"*Meurtre, meurtre! Mon Dieu—meurtre,
meurtre!*"—(Murder, murder! my God—
murder, murder!)—was shrieked by some one
in agonising accents.

It was the voice of Jeanette, who had,
according to instructions, gone to call Duromme.   Receiving no response to her repeated
knocks, she opened the chamber door.

The sight she saw was an awful one.
There lay the ghastly corpse of Duromme,
with a dagger sticking in his heart.

CHAPTER XXII.

THE ACCUSATION.

" Foul deeds will rise
Though all the earth o'erwhelms them to men's eyes ;
For murder, though it have no tongue, will speak
With most miraculous organ."

Shakespeare.

IT was too true. There lay Duromme's body stark and stiff. According to the diagnosis of a surgeon, who was sent for, Duromme had been dead some five or six hours. His death had been instantaneous. But where was Monsieur l'assassin? The police were called.

There was the bloody dagger, but it, as yet at any rate, told no tale. It was handed to the chef de police, who examined it, and found an earl's coronet engraven on the hilt. This was something to begin with.

" Will messieurs explain who they are, and

what is their business in France?" politely
asks the chef.

Lord Charles explains that he is nephew
of the Earl of Eglinton, and is travelling in
search of a missing young lady; while his
companion is his attendant.

"And see you, Monsieur, that there is an
Earl's coronet on the hilt of this dagger?"

Lord Charles starts suddenly with un-
feigned amazement. He recognises the
dagger as one belonging to his uncle.

"And, mademoiselle; what may be her
business? Why is she travelling with two
young men?"

It is explained that she is intended to be
tire-woman and companion of the young lady
as soon as she is found.

"Messieurs and mademoiselle must consider
themselves under arrest. I am sorry, but it
is my duty," said the chef.

"Good God!" exclaimed Lord Charles,
"the murdered man was our friend, and
assisting us in the search for the missing
lady."

That mattered not. The dead man's papers showed that he was a Frenchman, while the others of the party were English.

Then there was the damning evidence of the coroneted dagger.

" But surely you will not arrest the young woman ? " asked Lord Charles anxiously.

" My duty, Monsieur ; I must perform my duty," and he raised his kepi with the most extreme politeness.

And Lord Charles Montgomery, Guy Gordon, and Jean Graham were forthwith lodged in the fortress at Lille.

During the day several scraps of evidence turned up in their favour. The watch-dog had been poisoned, and the outer gate of the hotel, that had been carefully bolted the night before, had been opened from the inside.

But strongest evidence of all in their favour was the fact that a pair of strange shoes had been found at the end of the wooden gallery nearest the outer gate.

These shoes would not fit any one of the

three prisoners. Thus it might have been
that the murderer in his haste, after com-
mitting the foul deed, had left the shoes
behind him.

Moreover, and again in their favour, in a
few days it was found out that a foot-sore
little old man, with a slouched hat, a loose
cloak, and walking barefoot, purchased a
pair of shoes from a *cordonnier* at a village
some ten miles from Lille, on the old road to
Paris.

Finally, the police were aware—in such
cases the French police are always aware—
that a young lady with an attendant had
passed through Lille a day or two before.

The members of the French police force
are like the celebrated parrot—they say very
little, but they think a very great deal
indeed.

As is usual in France, when a crime is
committed, the most minute inquiries were
made all over the country, but nothing could
be found respecting the old man who had
bought the shoes. He appeared to be as

mysterious as the murder itself. Not a clue could be got as to his whereabouts.

Day by day the mystery became more and more perplexing. Lille and the surrounding district rang with the story of the murder, and public opinion was about equally divided as to the guilt or innocence of the two handsome young Scotsmen and their still handsomer female companion.

Naturally, Jean Graham had the worst of the unfortunate position. Lord Charles and Guy bore up manfully under the circumstances ; but poor Jean spent her lonely days in weeping. Fortunately they were not treated with anything like severity in the fortress.

After all possible evidence had been collected, it was announced, as was then customary in every *cause celèbre*, that the accused should be taken to Paris for trial. This was accordingly done, and in a few days our three unfortunate travellers found themselves in the celebrated prison now called Mazas.

It is curious to observe the avidity with which the public seize upon and discuss the details of certain murders. Rush, Palmer, Madeline Smith, Jessie M'Lachlan, and Dr Pritchard were all, excepting Miss Smith, convicted of revolting murders; and during each of the trials public excitement was at its very highest. Yet, during the period over which these murders stretched there were quite as revolting ones committed without anything more than the slightest notice being taken of them.

In Paris the excitement concerning the Lille murder was very great. Gabrielle, like others, heard of it, and for obvious reasons became much excited over the details. She asked and readily obtained permission to visit the prisoners before the trial.

Accordingly, Gabrielle made the necessary arrangements, and one bright morning found her within the frowning walls of the gloomy Mazas—next to the Bastille, the most famous, or rather infamous, prison in France.

As the huge key turned in the lock of the cell in which her lover was confined, Gabrielle felt so faint that she would have fallen on the cold, hard pavement had she not been supported by the strong arm of the kindly-hearted turnkey.

Then she entered hastily, followed by the silent official.

After a fond embrace, Gabrielle Stuart and Charles Montgomery looked at each other for some time without speaking.

" I am aware, my dearest Charles, that you know nought of that foul murder. But *I* know," she whispered.

He looked thunderstruck.

" Yes; and God in His good time will avenge it thoroughly."

" Thanks be to the Almighty !" exclaimed Charles. " There is thus some hope that we may soon get out of this terrible position."

" The case will go to trial, but the best advocates will plead your cause."

" Once more, thanks be to the Almighty

for his goodness. But who, may I ask, was
Charles Duromme?"

Hear Gabrielle's tears fell fast. After the
burst of grief had somewhat abated, she
sobbingly answered—

"Alas! alas! you must await for a time
that information. God help us! And you
are undergoing, my dearest Charles, all this
terrible suffering for my sake!"

.   .   .   .   .

Gabrielle's interview with Jean Graham
was also of a most affecting character. Poor
Jean completely broke down when she saw
Gabrielle. But her's were tears of joy. And
before Gabrielle left the prison, Jean was
buoyed up still more strongly than she had
hitherto been by the consolation that is ever
derived from conscious innocence.

The visit to Guy Gordon was the least
affecting of the three. Guy was, of course,
more than glad to see Gabrielle, and his great
hope was that the trial would come on soon,
as he felt sure they would all be freely
acquitted. He had just, he told Gabrielle,

composed a little song to Jean Graham, and
at the time of her call he was trying to sing
it to an old tune.

Perhaps it may not be out of place to give
here Guy's maiden and prison effort.

MY BONNIE JEAN.

I've lo'ed thee lang, I've lo'ed thee weel,
How I ha'e lo'ed thee nane can feel :
I'll lo'e thee still my bonnie queen,
I'll lo'e for aye my bonnie Jean.

When absent thou art ever near,
When present thou art still more dear,
No other face or form I ween,
'Can match wi' thine, my bonnie Jean.

When adverse storms my bosom chill'd,
When losses made me oft self-will'd,
Then my sole solace e'er hast been
My dearest love, my bonnie Jean.

Still, as the tide of life rolls on,
We'll talk o' happy hours long gone,
And from the past sweet pleasures glean—
My heart, my soul, my bonnie Jean.

Writing a song when in prison on a charge
of murder looks not a little unlike dancing
over a volcano ; but it is a fact that some of

the best work of great authors has been done in positions of difficulty. Brave men are always cool in presence of danger.

Guy Gordon had not a sufficient appreciation of how easy it is to get into a French prison, and how difficult it is to get out. It has, in later days, become a standing joke in France that the difficult feat has been accomplished only by Marshal Bazaine and the devil!

For the foreigner in France there is always plenty of liberty—that is, if the foreigner interferes not with French politics. But I have known the case of an Englishman who, having resided fifteen years in France, took the unpardonable liberty of taking part in an election squabble.

On the night of the day on which he had so interfered, and while he was sitting quietly with his wife in a theatre, a mouchard gave him twenty-four hours' notice to quit France. And he was forced to go.

CHAPTER XXIII.

THE TRIAL.

"Innocence unmoved
At a false accusation, doth the more
Confirm itself, and guilt is best discovered
By its own fears."
Beaumont and Fletcher.

PARIS was gay. Paris is always gay, excepting when the blood of the tiger-monkey is up. The Parisians can be gay at a trial or at an execution, at a marriage or at a funeral. They not long ago cheered lustily the Imperial eagle; they are at present fondling the tricolor; next year they may be doing homage to the white flag and the golden lilies of the Bourbons.

Although now it would seem that the "Drapeau Blanc" has but a very poor chance of again floating in France; let us, however, fondly trust that the "Drapeau Rouge" never will—at anyrate with the sad surroundings it has formerly and repeatedly exhibited. We do not wish again to hear that dreadful cry, "Ca ira! les aristocrats à la lanterne—seront pendus!" (Hang the aristocrats to the lamposts!)

Even the Palais de Justice was gay. Richly-attired ladies occupied the front seats, and chatted merrily with their gentlemen friends. What cared they for three fellow-creatures charged with murder? Were they not aliens, and was not their victim a Frenchman? The sacred body of a Frenchman, even to the present day, must not be personally touched in the slightest degree with impunity. Even the most trifling assault is always punished by imprisonment as well as fine.

At last the accused are placed in the dock; the Public Prosecutor takes his place in a little pulpit-looking box at the side of the Judges' bench; and the Judges enter and take their seats under a life-size representaion of our Saviour on the Cross. The jury are sworn and the trial proceeds, as has long been the case in France, by the Judges interrogating the prisoners.

Jean Graham is first examined as to her suspicions that the party was being watched by a stranger. But what could the stranger watch? and why were you, mademoiselle, with the party? (This is how the Judge proceeds, even after the accused have been before a Judge d'Instruction, and the same questions put and answered. Thus, by making double statements, a French prisoner is often convicted out of his own mouth.)

Jean Graham can only weep and state that she knows nothing more about the matter than that she noticed that she and her companions were being followed by some one who appeared to have an object in watching their movements.

Lord Charles Montgomery, interrogated as to the ownership off the dagger, frankly admitted that it was the property of his uncle, the Earl of Eglinton, who would come forward that day and make an explanation as to how it had got out of his possession.

Guy Gordon, who seemed the most uncon-
cerned person in the Court, had nothing to
say further than that he heard what he
fancied was a sound of distress during the
night, and that he rushed out, sword in hand,
and found Lord Charles Montgomery, also
carrying his sword, on the gallery of the hotel.

Simple as Guy's statement looked, it caused
considerable sensation in Court. Lord Charles
was again interrogated.

"And what, Monsieur, were you doing on
the gallery during the dead of night?"

"The same reason that took my friend
there took me. I fancied I heard a stifled
cry of deep distress."

The Judges looked significantly at each
other. It was plain that this evidence was
going against the male prisoners, so the
Public Prosecutor here withdrew the charge
against Jean Graham, and she was removed
from the dock.

The testimony of the hotel-keeper at Calais,
the testimony of the hotel-keeper at Lille, the
testimony of the police at the fortress—all

these testimonies were then recorded duly, and noted by the three Judges and the Public Prosecutor.

The chef of the police at Lille was still further examined, but he threw no more light on the matter of the murder. Monsieur le Chef had seen the dead body and the dagger; he had seen the blood oozing from the wound; he had seen the accused persons; but he could form no opinion on the murder. To Messieurs les Judges he could state no more. To him (the chef) the whole affair was most mysterious. Still it was a murder —a foul murder—and he deemed it to be his simple duty to put the whole case before the Court as a crime that ought to be thoroughly investigated.

The chef de police concluded his evidence by stating that every endeavour had been made to find the man who bought the shoes from the *cordonnier* about ten miles from Lille, but he had not been discovered.

Then the Public Prosecutor summed up for a conviction. His theory was, that some international dispute had arisen, and that, carrying out the wellknown antipathy of the English to the French, the two foreigners had arisen stealthily during the night and foully slain the man they believed to be their natural enemy.

It was here pointed out by the chief *avocat* for the defence that the accused were Scotchmen, not Englishmen, and that fact made a material difference, seeing that the French and the Scotch were allies rather than enemies.

The Judges admitted that such was the case. The brave Scotch had ever been the allies of the French. (And now a hum in favour of the prisoners was plainly heard in Court.)

The first witness for the defence was the Earl of Eglinton, who stated that the dagger produced was lost by him, or had been stolen from his tent, at the great Restoration Tourney held in the city of Glasgow.

Next came Mr Godfrey Marling, who clearly proved that Monsieur Duromme had specially requested permission to join the expedition that had proceeded in search of the young lady who had so suddenly and mysteriously disappeared.

Then came a hush of expectation and curiosity. A young lady, dressed in the deepest mourning, and closely veiled, came in front of the bar and desired to be sworn.

Raising her veil she disclosed features of transcendent loveliness, although showing marked traces of deep grief.

"Your name, Mademoiselle?" asked the presiding Judge.

"Gabrielle Stuart de Guise, commonly called Gabrielle Stuart," she answered with an amount of grace and dignity that seemed marvellous in one so young.

("Stuart de Guise!" was whispered over the Court; "one of the most ancient families in France.")

"Your nation?"

"I was born in France, but I was brought up and educated in Scotland."

"What know you of the two prisoners at the bar?"

"One is my friend; the other is my affianced," and a modest maidenly blush overspread her pale cheeks.

"What knew you of the murdered man?" was the next question.

"He was my maternal uncle!"

And as Gabrielle shed tears, a sound of sympathy was audible throughout the Court.

There is no middling course with the French. They are either very cruel or very kind, either sympathetic or fiendish.

"How comes it, Mademoiselle, that the name of the deceased was Duromme? Are you not aware that it is an infringement of the law of France to assume a name other than the one in which you have been baptised?"

"Political and financial difficulties caused my grandfather to change his name; but he received State permission so to do."

"Your answers, Mademoiselle," said the presiding Judge, "are thoroughly explicit and satisfactory."

Then the principal *avocat* for the defence

requested that the dagger with which the murder had been committed should be handed to the witness.

Gabrielle shuddered as she took the still gory weapon in her trembling hand.

" Where saw you that dagger last ?" asked the learned counsel.

" On a small Scottish island named Lady Isle, situated in the Firth of Clyde."

" In whose possession was the weapon ? "

" In the possession of a sworn enemy of my poor uncle."

At this point the now agitated Gabrielle gave a perceptible shudder.

" The name and designation of the possessor ? "

" Lord Kennedy of Greenan."

" There was no possibility of the weapon coming into the possession of your un-fortunate uncle or the accused ? "

" None. The dagger was taken away from the island before my uncle left with the expedition which had been arranged to search for me."

This finished the evidence.

Once more the Public Prosecutor demanded a conviction. He scouted the statements of Gabrielle as being theatrical clap-trap, got up to throw dust in the eyes of the jury.

A French Public Prosecutor is actually much more severe than a Scotch one. And that is saying a good deal.

Just as a French advocate will use stronger terms than will a Scotch one in his attempts to clear his client.

Why, it is not long since I heard at a trial, in the Palace de Justice, Paris, Maitre Lachaud declare, on his word of honour, his belief that it was utterly impossible for an officer of the English army to tell an untruth !

The chief counsel for the defence then addressed the jury. He was as eloquent as was a celebrated Scottish advocate—now the Lord Justice-General of Scotland—in a murder case of the present day, and some of his words were almost similar in their character and solemnity.

"Gentlemen of the Jury,—The charge

against the prisoners is murder, and the punishment of murder is death. That simple statement is sufficient to suggest to us the awful solemnity of the case which has brought you and me face to face. But, gentlemen, there are peculiarities in the present case of so singular and strange a kind, and there is an air of romance and mystery in it from beginning to end—something so touching and truthful in the age, sex, and statements of the last witness—that I have no conscientious scruple in asking you to thoroughly acquit the persons now charged before you."

The jury were a long time in retirement, and that seemed ominous for the accused. After an hour's absence, however, they returned to Court, and gave the then French and now Scotch verdict of

" Not Proven."

Then came thunders of applause from the excited multitude. The speech for the defence had taken them completely by storm, and Charles Montgomery and Guy Gordon, in passing out of the Court, were here and there not a little annoyed at being fondly embraced by over-zealous Frenchmen!

This is a style of embrace I could never take to in France. My want of experience debars me from describing the sensation of being kissed by a Frenchwoman; but a Frenchman—*Jamais!*

.   .   .   .   .

But the eventful proceedings of that eventful day were not yet done.

The relations and friends of Gabrielle, confident in an acquittal of the accused, had arranged that a thanksgiving service should take place at the Cathedral of Notre Dame.

Accordingly a large party assembled in the ancient building.

First there was a procession of priests, then the venerable Archbishop of Paris knelt at the top of the altar steps, and anon the organ pealed forth the glorious tune to the words, "We praise Thee, O God."

But scarcely had the choir got over the words, "*Te Deum Laudamus*," when an excited priest, with a glittering short sword in his hand, rushed behind the archbishop and buried the weapon up to the hilt in the prelate's body.

The old man, without a groan, fell down the altar steps stone dead.

Then occurred to Gabrielle the gipsy's prophecy—

"Thy wedding will be brought about by death."

"O, God!" exclaimed Gabrielle, "spare, O spare Thy servants. Take me away, but, Lord, do Thou spare them."

END OF VOL. I.

THOS. GRAY AND CO., GEORGE STREET, EDINBURGH.

"Messrs Dunn & Wright, in issuing such
Literature, are doing a good work."
—*United Presbyterian Magazine.*

WORKS PUBLISHED

BY

DUNN & WRIGHT,

GLASGOW AND LONDON.

London Agents—ALFRED PALMER & SON,

12 PATERNOSTER ROW.

"Messrs Dunn & Wright, Glasgow, the well-
known Printers, have hit upon the happy idea
of publishing a series of small volumes, full of
interest to the general reader."
—*Border Advertiser.*

9/82.

NEW WORKS AND NEW EDITIONS

PUBLISHED BY

DUNN & WRIGHT,

176 BUCHANAN STREET, AND 102 STIRLING ROAD,

GLASGOW.

Crown 8vo, with frontispiece, cloth, gilt title, 3/6.

K N O X

AND THE

REFORMATION TIMES IN SCOTLAND.

BY JEAN L. WATSON, EDINBURGH.

PREFACE BY REV. ROBERT MUIR, HAWICK.

"We cordially recommend this book for a wide circulation."—*United Presbyterian Magazine.*

"We recommend it *very specially* to the attention of teachers, and all who are responsible for the education of the young."—*Glasgow Sabbath School Magazine.*

"The book before us deals with the very grandest period of all Scottish history, and with one of the greatest of all Scotchmen."—*Literary World.*

"The publication of such a book is always opportune: to many it will be especially so at the present time."—*Glasgow Herald.*

"This is a cheap, compact, and most readable summary of what concerns the mass of *Scotch* people, especially to know about *their* Reformer."—*The Family Treasury.*

"To any one anxious to get a knowledge of Reformation Times, this book will be found very useful."—*League Journal.*

"This book is exceedingly opportune, and should be extensively read and circulated by all true friends of Protestantism."—*Christian Union.*

"This is one of the most useful and popular series of volumes."—*Daily Review.*

"Parents could not do better than make their children early acquainted with the contents of this volume."—*Haddingtonshire Courier.*

"A vivid picture of the one Scotch epoch of 'world interest.'"—*Glasgow Herald.*

"Knox was the life and soul of the great Reformation in Scotland.—*Preface.*

Foolscap 8vo, 320 pp., cloth, gilt title, 5/-.

GREYCLIFF HALL,

AND OTHER POEMS.

By ALICE PRINGLE, Auchterarder.

"There is enough of mystery to charm the greedy reader on to the very close. After perusing the volume, our readers will thank us for calling their attention to it."—*Berwick Advertiser.*

Foolscap 8vo, 292 pp., Illustrated, cloth, bevelled boards, gilt title, 3/6.

INSCRIPTIONS ON THE
TOMBSTONES AND MONUMENTS
ERECTED IN
MEMORY OF THE COVENANTERS.

By JAMES GIBSON, Esq., Liverpool,

Editor of "Burns' Calendar," "Burns' Birthday Book," etc.

"Those who wish to read the tale of the Covenanters' graves cannot do better than procure this volume."—*Liverpool Mercury.*

"A neat and handy edition."—*Glasgow Herald.*

"The most concise and comprehensive compendium of the Covenanting period we have ever seen."—*Stirling Observer.*

"This is sure to become a standard work."—*Freeman.*

"Every available source of information has been consulted which could throw light upon the names of the Martyrs."—*Preface.*

"The most complete record of the Martyr-stones ever yet published."—*Ardrossan and Saltcoats Herald.*

"The volume deserves a place in every library."—*Kirkcudbrightshire Advertiser.*

"This cannot fail to be profitable reading to all lovers of wholesome books."—*Hawick Express.*

"The volume is prettily got up, and illustrated by several wood engravings."—*Bookseller.*

Foolscap 8vo, 534 pp., cloth, gilt title, 2/6.

THE SCOTS WORTHIES.

By JOHN HOWIE, of LOCHGOIN.

"We heartily commend it to the notice of Ministers and Sunday School Teachers, as a book for the times."—*Christian Union.*

"We cordially commend the book to our readers, and we are persuaded they will peruse it eagerly."—*Berwickshire News.*

"This is a very handsome volume, beautiful in type, chaste in binding, and cheap in price."—*Advance.*

"A work which contains biographical sketches of the leading personages who struggled and died for the Covenanted work of Reformation, and which has obtained an almost unrivalled popularity in the rural districts of Scotland."—HUGH MACDONALD.—(See "*Rambles Round Glasgow,*" page 152.)

HUGH MACDONALD'S WORKS.

Crown 8vo, cloth, gilt title, Illustrated, 3/6 each.

RAMBLES ROUND GLASGOW,

AND

DAYS AT THE COAST.

WITH A MOST INTERESTING MEMOIR.

"Latest and best editions."—*Evening Citizen.*

"These are new and improved editions of charming books. We cordially commend these volumes, and wish for them a wide circulation."—*Daily Mail.*

Crown 8vo, 400 pp., handsomely bound, cloth, gilt title, 3/6.

ROUND ABOUT FALKIRK.

By ROBERT GILLESPIE.

"Much that is both interesting and instructive. The work will be read with great relish."—*Falkirk Herald.*

"A most useful companion to the stranger and tourist."—*Stirling Observer.*

"This is one of a class of books that we all like to read."—*Stirling Journal*

"The author's descriptions are written well and tastefully."—*Daily Mail.*

"An interesting book, in which the author shows considerable familiarity with the historical and antiquarian landmarks about Stirling and Linlithgow."—*Scotsman.*

"The work is enlivened with many curious anecdotes, illustrative of Scottish character."—*Edinburgh Courant.*

"We recommend this work. It comprises good information, and is written in felicitous style."—*Glasgow Herald.*

"Our author is most pleasant, sprightly, and communicative; always brief, and rich in allusive stories."—*Glasgow League Journal.*

"Has what guide-books do not ordinarily meddle with—glimpses and pictures of social life."—*Daily Review.*

"A large amount of highly interesting and valuable information contained in this delightful volume."—*Airdrie Advertiser.*

"The author is a genuine Falkirk 'bairn'—an enthusiastic nature-lover, and thoroughly patriotic."—*Weekly Standard.*

"A book which one would like to have in his hand when visiting any of the localities described."—*Dumbarton Herald.*

"A very interesting volume. A visitor to Falkirk could not have a better guide."—*Dumfries Standard.*

Crown 8vo, Illustrated cover, 1/-; cloth, gilt title, 2/-; fine thick paper edition, gilt edges, frontispiece, 3/-.

Rev. ALEX. PEDEN (the Prophet),

AND

Rev. JAMES RENWICK:

THEIR LIFE AND TIMES.

By JEAN L. WATSON, EDINBURGH.

WITH INTRODUCTORY ESSAY ON SCOTTISH NATIONALITY

By the Rev. JOHN KER, D.D.,

SYDNEY PLACE U.P. CHURCH, GLASGOW.

"I have read this book with much interest and satisfaction. The Preface by Dr Ker is very admirable, and will do much good. I trust it may be widely circulated and carefully pondered."—Rev. JAS. BEGG, D.D., *Edinburgh.*

"Young men who are forming libraries of their own cannot do better than add this volume to their collection. The essay by the Rev. Dr Ker on Scottish Nationality is a noble introduction to the book. We trust that this volume will have a large circulation."—*Glasgow Young Men's Magazine.*

"In this volume we have beauty, utility, and cheapness combined. The introduction by Dr John Ker is a piece of as fine and just historical writing as we have anywhere seen. We heartily commend this handsome volume."—*Advance.*

"Our readers will be glad to make the acquaintance of this very attractive and interesting volume, containing memoirs of Alexander Peden and James Renwick. Dr Ker's introductory chapter examines into the origin and development of Scottish Nationality, and is highly instructive and suggestive. We strongly recommend the book."—*Glasgow Sabbath School Magazine.*

"We welcome the volume before us. Perhaps two better specimens of our covenanting forefathers could not have been selected."—*League Journal.*

"This volume is very seasonable at the present time, when the question of Disestablishment is much before the public."—*Berwick Advertiser.*

"Very complete and concise, written in a graphic style, and shows thorough appreciation of Peden's character and principles."—*Kelso Chronicle.*

"Much care has been bestowed on the revision of those portions of the writings of Peden and Renwick that are given in this volume."—Rev. JOHN KER, D.D.

"The story is fitted to thrill every reader's heart, and it is well and pleasantly told."—*Belfast Witness.*

Crown 8vo, Illustrated cover, 1/-; cloth, gilt title, 2/-; fine thick paper edition, gilt edges, engraved Portrait, 3/-.

BROWNIE OF BODSBECK,

AND OTHER TALES,

BY THE "ETTRICK SHEPHERD,"

WITH BIOGRAPHICAL SKETCH

BY LAURENCE ANDERSON, ESQ., MOFFAT.

"Hogg gave himself up to the genius of romance, and luxuriated in fairy visions. If, as has been stated, 'The Queen's Wake' is his most popular poem, 'The Brownie of Bodsbeck' is his favourite story."—*L. Anderson, Moffat.*

Crown 8vo, Illustrated cover, 1/-; cloth, gilt title, 2/-; fine thick paper edition, gilt edges, 3/-.

THE TWO GUTHRIES:

THEIR LIFE AND TIMES;

OR, SKETCHES OF THE COVENANTS.

BY JEAN L. WATSON, EDINBURGH.

"The author's sketch of the Covenants is simply a great literary treat, as interesting as the most fascinating of our Scottish tales, yet breathing throughout the hallowed and ennobling spirit of these heroic, patriotic, and eminently pious men, 'The Scottish Worthies.' We very heartily commend this volume to our readers."—*The People's Journal.*

Crown 8vo, Illustrated cover, 1/-; cloth, gilt title, 2/-; fine thick paper edition, gilt edges, frontispiece, 3/-.

COTTAGERS OF GLENBURNIE.

By Mrs ELIZABETH HAMILTON,

AND SELECTIONS FROM

LIGHTS AND SHADOWS OF SCOTTISH LIFE,

WITH PREFATORY NOTE

By JEAN L. WATSON, EDINBURGH.

"This is an interesting story, which conveys lessons that many house-wives in our large towns, as well as in rural districts, need."—*Scottish Congregational Magazine.*

"As a picture of Scottish village life in the last century, the book is unequalled and inimitable. Infinite amusement, and no little instruction, may be derived from a perusal of this work."—*Kelso Chronicle.*

"We are gratified to notice a new edition of this original and well-told tale, which has perhaps done more to improve the dwellings and habits of our villagers than all our sanitary inspectors."—*League Journal.*

"For the long winter nights or summer evenings this is most useful and healthy literature. A large circulation would do much to entertain and instruct a vast number who have few books. We cordially thank the enterprising publishers for this beautiful and cheap edition."—*The Advance.*

"This is a well written tale, evidently intended for the benefit of the working classes. It is also a very suitable prize for young people."—*Free Press.*

Crown 8vo, Illustrated cover, 1/-; cloth, gilt title, 2/-; fine thick paper edition, gilt edges, 3/-.

THE QUEEN'S WAKE,

AND OTHER POEMS.

BY THE "ETTRICK SHEPHERD."

PREFATORY NOTE

By JEAN L. WATSON, EDINBURGH.

"Most great works have an interesting history. 'The Queen's Wake' has a particularly rich one. It was not only the author's most successful work, but it was his only great work that could have securely established his literary position in the world."—*Moffat Times.*

"This poem is full of rich gems which have rarely been surpassed."—*Free Press.*

"A nice edition for the pocket."—*Sheriff Veitch.*

"As a lyric poet, James Hogg is second to Robert Burns. His humorous songs kept the famous meetings at Ambrose's in a roar; his pastoral lyrics, popular in the drawing-room and at the cottar's fireside, have given a poetical beauty to the rural pastimes and loves of our peasantry; his Jacobite lays have excited and kept up a sympathy with the misfortunes of the Royal house of Stuart, whose history has a melancholy interest; and his patriotic songs, if sung on the eve of a battle, would be more effective than ten thousand men."—*L. Anderson, Esq.*

Crown 8vo, Illustrated cover, 1/-; cloth, gilt title, 2/-; fine thick paper edition, gilt edges, 3/-.

RINGAN GILHAIZE;
Or, THE TIMES OF THE COVENANTERS.

By JOHN GALT.

Crown 8vo, Illustrated cover, 1/-; cloth, gilt title, 2/-; fine thick paper edition, gilt edges, 3/-.

POLLOK'S TALES OF THE COVENANTERS;

COMPRISING

HELEN OF THE GLEN, RALPH GEMMELL, AND THE

PERSECUTED FAMILY.

WITH LIFE OF THE AUTHOR

By JEAN L. WATSON, EDINBURGH.

"Pollok's 'Tales of the Covenanters' have long been favourite reading with young people in Scotland. Older people will find them not unworthy of their perusal in their more mature years. Pollok's views of Gospel truths are wonderfully full and correct. Miss Watson's 'Life' tells with much interest the story of the poet's career."—*Reformed Presbyterian Magazine.*

"There is no need to specify the contents and nature of these 'Tales.' The book is so well known and so universally read that nothing further is required than to mention that a *new edition has appeared.* This is a class of literature that the rising generation should know."—*Advance.*

"Thirty or forty years ago there was hardly a more popular book among intelligent boys than a little volume containing 'Helen of the Glen,' 'Ralph Gemmell,' and 'The Persecuted Family.' If any juvenile library does not contain these Tales, this volume should be at once secured. It is sure to furnish beneficial mental food for the young."—*Kelso Chronicle.*

"We welcome such works as these. Pollok's 'Tales' and his grand poem, 'The Course of Time,' ought to be in every house. This edition is a marvel of cheapness."—*Scottish Congregational Magazine.*

"In these days of light literature a perusal of Pollok's Tales may furnish a pleasant antidote to much that is frivolous and pernicious."—*League Journal.*

"Pollok's 'Tales of the Covenanters' were among our earliest Sabbath-school prizes, and their perusal was to us a source of deep and tearful interest."—HUGH MACDONALD.—(See "*Rambles Round Glasgow*," page 174.)

"This covenanting story has had a wide popularity."—*L. Anderson, Esq.*

Crown 8vo, Illustrated cover, 1/-; cloth, gilt title, 2/-; fine thick paper edition, gilt edges, 3/-.

THE COURSE OF TIME,

By ROBERT POLLOK, M.A.,

WITH PREFATORY NOTE
By JEAN L. WATSON, EDINBURGH.

"We welcome such works as these, which we should like to be read by every succeeding generation."—*Scottish Congregational Magazine.*

"Pollok's 'Course of Time' has taken its place in the literature of our country, and needs no commendation. Miss Watson's Preface is well and gracefully written, and sketches the leading events in the poet's life. This edition is a marvel of cheapness."—*Reformed Presbyterian Magazine.*

"The 'Course of Time' is one of the poems that posterity will not willingly let die, and we cordially welcome this edition of Pollok's immortal poem; it is a handsome volume."—*Kelso Chronicle.*

"'The Course of Time' will remain a standing monument to the intellectual power and sanctified genius of one who passed away at the early age of 26 years. The present edition will make a handsome gift-book."—*League Journal.*

"We commend the book for Sunday reading."—*Daily Review.*

"This new issue is an evidence of the continued appreciation in which this 'noble poem' is held. A neat edition, tastefully finished, and containing a 'Prefatory Note' of great interest."—*Advance.*

Crown 8vo, Illustrated cover, 1/-; cloth, gilt title, 2/-; fine thick paper edition, gilt edges, 3/-.

ANNALS OF THE PARISH,

AND THE

AYRSHIRE LEGATEES.

By JOHN GALT.

WITH LIFE OF THE AUTHOR,
By JEAN L. WATSON, EDINBURGH.

"Mr Galt, who was a native of Irvine, Ayrshire, chose that district as the scene of the stories which form the present volume. 'The Annals of the Parish' may be considered to be in relation to Scotland what the 'Vicar of

Wakefield' is to England. These 'Annals of the Parish' present the simple manners and homely ways of the villagers of a century ago, and their relations to the parish minister, in a most interesting way, and introduces phases of thought and peculiarities of expression which have almost become extinct."—*Daily Review.*

"Miss Watson's 'Life of the Author' is interesting and well told. The volume is carefully got up, and is worthy a place on the drawing-room table."—*Border Advertiser.*

"Well worthy of perusal, and we have no doubt that it will be extensively circulated."—*Free Press.*

Crown 8vo, Illustrated cover, 1/-; cloth, gilt title, 2/-; fine thick paper edition; gilt edges, 3/-.

THE DISRUPTION:

A TALE OF TRYING TIMES.

By WILLIAM CROSS, Esq., GLASGOW.

THIRD EDITION. REVISED BY THE AUTHOR.

"Not only as an entertaining narrative, but as containing many reliable references to the quick-spreading events of the Disruption era, served up in a thorough attractive form. Around the great events of Disruption history, which to the popular mind are as rough and barren of interest as a boulder on a hill side, the author has planted the fresh and attractive blossoms of literary gracefulness, power of description, and knowledge of human nature, so that at each successive step one is tempted to linger and ponder over the great things that were done in those days. We would particularly recommend this book."—*Daily Mail.*

"A cheap but tastefully got up volume."—*Renfrewshire Independent.*

"Mr Cross has adopted the vehicle of fictitious narrative to convey to us the essence of what really happened in the great conflict."—*Border Advertiser.*

"A very clear and interesting story. We can remember the eagerness with which it was read when it was originally published. The tale will always be read with pleasure, as a faithful description of the times of the Disruption, and as providing graphic delineations of Scottish character in its many phases. There is in it capital specimens of genuine humour. Many of the scenes are given with great vividness of expression. The book is handsomely got up, both in binding and letterpress."—*League Journal.*

"A work of real merit and absorbing interest. It deserves an extensive circulation, and we have no doubt it will find its way into thousands of homes. It is a book for all times."—*The Alderman.*

[Unabridged Edition ; 120th Thousand.]

256 pp., Royal 32mo, Illustrated cover, 2d; cloth, gilt title, Portrait, Biography, and 32 full-page Illustrations, 6d.

PILGRIM'S PROGRESS.

This Edition has had a very large and ready sale. A very suitable book to put into the hands of Sabbath School and other children.

Crown 8vo, Illustrated cover, 1/-; *cloth, gilt title.* 2/-; *fine thick paper edition, gilt edges,* 3/-.

THE STORY OF
A DISPUTED SETTLEMENT

AFTER THE DISRUPTION;

OR,

LOVE, LAW, AND THEOLOGY.

BY

ALEXANDER MACDONALD, Writer, Glasgow.

₊ *Large Type Library Edition,* 608 *pages, with* 14 *full-page Illustrations, plain,* 4/6.

"Very lively and interesting."—*Right Hon. W. E. Gladstone.*

"A very appropriate study at the present time."—*Earl of Stair.*

"A new and well illustrated edition. We have read this book with combined instruction and amusement."—*Border Advertiser.*

"We would most heartily commend this work as worthy of the earnest and careful perusal of our readers."—*Free Press.*

"This is substantially a good as it is a clever book. The author's style is always clear and vigorous; sometimes eloquent, never dull. We will not attempt an epitome of the story itself, but content ourselves with recommending its perusal to all who are interested in the working of Ecclesiastical Courts. There is not a dull page in the whole volume."—*Scotsman.*

"Here is an eminently amusing and clever book. To say so is to award high praise. It is wonderfully rich in good materials. Many of the characters are capitally drawn, with clear, bold, vivid touches, presenting a rare lucidness of outline, great force of colour, and graphic precision, which is really remarkable."—*N. B. Daily Mail.*

"Mr Macdonald treats the subject with great cleverness, and with an amount of racy and farcical humour that reminds one of Irish novelists of the type of Lover and Lever."—*Inverness Courier.*

Crown 8vo, Illustrated cover, 1/-; *cloth, gilt title,* 2/-; *fine thick paper edition, gilt edges,* 3/-.

A STUDENT'S ADVENTURES IN
TURKEY AND THE EAST.

BY

ALEXANDER MACDONALD, Writer, Glasgow.

"The student who is the hero has been compelled, by the pressure of circumstances, to enlist in the French Zouave regiment, in which he has won his way to a captaincy, and had some startling experiences in the Crimean war. These and some other 'Adventures' Mr Macdonald recounts with a dash and spirit which reminds the reader of Lever's earlier novels. There is not a dull page in this volume, which will be found full of interest to all who relish stories of intrigue and adventure."—*Scotsman.*

"The allusions to student life and old friends at the University will be very acceptable to our readers."—*Daily Mail.*

Foolscap 8vo, cloth, 1/6.

LIFE ON THE OCEAN.

BY

DAVID COWANS, LATE COMMANDER OF THE "FIERY CROSS."

"This book is altogether an entertaining one for young and old. Captain Cowans has many won lerful things to tell, but he is guiltless of spinning long yarns."—*Kelso Chronicle.*

"A neat and compact volume. We have much pleasure in commending it to the favourable attention of our readers."—*Greenock Telegraph.*

"Highly recommended by the Earl of Dufferin."—*Daily Mail.*

Foolscap 8vo, cloth, gilt title, 1/6.

THE YOUNG CHRISTIAN.

BY JACOB ABBOTT.

Foolscap 8vo, Cloth, with Portrait, 1/6.

ORATIONS, LECTURES, and ESSAYS.

BY RALPH WALDO EMERSON.

Uniform with the above, 1/6 each.

CRABBE'S TALES AND POEMS.

Two Vols.

Crown 8vo, cloth, 2/6.

SHINING WAIF.

BY

WILLIAM CANTON, GLASGOW.

"The author has made a pleasant addition to our literature."—*Glasgow Herald.*

"The author proves himself an adept at story-telling."—*Kelso Chronicle*

"It must be admitted that Messrs Dunn & Wright, in their 'Thistle' Series, have completely taken the lead of all others."—*Paisley Herald.*

"Thistle" Series.—The Poets.

Foolscap 8vo, 240 or 288 pages, printed on fine toned paper, in new clear type, Illustrated covers, 6d; handsomely bound, cloth, gilt title, 1/.

No. 1. LONGFELLOW'S POETICAL WORKS. With Portrait.
" 2. MOORE'S POETICAL WORKS. With Portrait.
" 3. BURNS'S POETICAL WORKS. With Portrait.
" 4. BYRON'S POETICAL WORKS. With Portrait.
" 5. SCOTT'S POETICAL WORKS. With Portrait.
" 6. COWPER'S POETICAL WORKS. With Portrait.
" 7. CAMPBELL'S POETICAL WORKS. With Portrait.
" 8. MILTON'S POETICAL WORKS. With Portrait.
" 9. TANNAHILL'S POETICAL WORKS (Memoir and Music). With Portrait.
" 10. MOTHERWELL'S POETICAL WORKS. With Portrait.
" 11. GOLDSMITH'S POETICAL WORKS. With Portrait.
" 12. BEATTIE'S POETICAL WORKS. With Portrait.

Other Works in Preparation.

————:o:————

Cloth, gilt title, 1/6; Illustrated cover, boards, 1/-.

Helen's Babies & Other People's Children.

BY HABBERTON.

————

Crown 8vo, Cloth, gilt title, 1/6.

GRANDFATHER'S LEGACY;

OR, THE BREWER'S FORTUNE.

BY MARY D. CHELLIS.

"This Temperance Story, written by a well-known American Author, gives a very good description of American Life. The lesson, that the liquor traffic bequeathes a fatal inheritance to many who may have made wealth by it, is also effectively enforced."—*League Journal.*

"*Thistle*" *Series.—Boys' Popular Tales.*

Foolscap 8vo, 240 pages, printed on fine paper, in new clear type Illustrated covers, 6d ; handsomely bound, cloth, gilt title, 1/-.

No. 1. ROBINSON CRUSOE; by DANIEL DEFOE.   Complete.

" 2. GULLIVER'S TRAVELS; by DEAN SWIFT.   Complete.

" 3. SWISS FAMILY ROBINSON.   Complete.

" 4. TALES FROM THE ARABIAN NIGHTS.   1st Series.

" 5.   Do.   do.   do.   2nd Series

" 6. WILLIS THE PILOT ; or, the Further Adventures of
the Swiss Crusoe Family.   Complete.

" 7. LIFE AND GARLAND OF ROBIN HOOD.

" 8. LIFE OF SIR WILLIAM WALLACE.

" 9. SANDFORD AND MERTON.

" 10. UNCLE TOM'S CABIN.

" 11. THE YOUNG ENGINEER OF THE LAKE SHORE
RAILWAY.

" 12. THE RIVAL ACADEMIES.

" 13. THE YOUNG CAPTAIN OF THE UCAGA STEAMER.

" 14. THE TWO BEARS ; or, the Young Skipper.

" 15. THE YOUNG PEACE MAKERS.

"*Thistle*" *Series.—Girls' Popular Tales.*

No. 1. THE WIDE, WIDE WORLD.

" 2. THE LAMPLIGHTER.

" 3. THE DAIRYMAN'S DAUGHTER.

" 4. THE BASKET OF FLOWERS, and other Tales.

" 5. THE PET LAMB, and other Tales.

" 6. SIMPLE SUSAN.

Other Works in Preparation.

——:o:——

Crown 8vo, cloth, gilt title, Frontispiece, 1/6.

PRINCE OF THE HOUSE OF DAVID.

Crown 8vo, paper cover, with eight full-page Illustrations, 1/-,

DOINGS IN DANBURY.

By THE DANBURY-NEWS MAN.

Popular editions.   Illustrated covers, Sixpence each.

HELEN'S BABIES.

OTHER PEOPLE'S CHILDREN.

MY MOTHER-IN-LAW.

HIS GRANDMOTHERS.

THAT HUSBAND OF MINE.

THAT WIFE OF MINE.

These interesting Works have met with immense success, *many thousands* of them having already been sold.

www.ingramcontent.com/pod-product-compliance
Lightning Source LLC
Chambersburg PA
CBHW030621030726
47497CB00006B/1580